Praise for *Gravity Doesn't Lie*:

"Part Blade Runner, part Chinatown, and completely its own thing, *Gravity Doesn't Lie* is a fast and fun dive into a dystopian solar system."

– M. V. Prindle, author of Bob the Wizard

Advance praise for *Atmosphere Meltdown* ...

"As per last time, **I couldn't put it down** (and the girl in the cupboard did not disappoint)!"

"I really enjoy these stories, they bring me back to my misspent youth. I thought this was a strong sequel, and I can't wait to see what's next!"

- D Berrington, Beta Reader

"I really enjoyed *Atmosphere Meltdown* and look forward to seeing how this story and world evolves over the series. Book two felt like a departure from book one in the best way. Where *Gravity Doesn't Lie* was a planet hopping adventure to rescue a damsel in distress, this story is one of rising tensions of class and ideology."

"the spaghetti western of sci-fi noir"

- K Moore, Editor

GRAVITY DOESN'T LIE

TRIGGER JONES

Gravity Doesn't Lie
a Joe Drive space noir

Paperback original published by Twintree Books / January 2023

ISBN: 978-1-7771335-2-8
Also available in ebook

Cover design: MiblArt Designs

Printed in the USA

Twintree
Books

Dedication

This book is dedicated to all reluctant heroes
who take action anyway

Chapter 1

She stood on the landing inside the door to Stony's Bar and Grill, simple but perfect in white blouse and blue denim, looking like everything the bar wasn't. Elegant. Refined. Graceful, even standing still. Definitely Elite. And, barely concealed beneath the surface, desperate.

Please let her be lost, Joe thought.

A twilight hush fell over the room like a wave. She scanned the bar, locked her gaze on him, and flowed down the three steps to the stool next to his at the bar. "Are you Joe Drive?" she asked.

"Would it help if I said no?" He knew her voice from the holo reels, the same smooth alto that went with one of the most recognizable faces in the Solar System.

A trace of smile breezed across her face and was gone. "Probably not. I need your help, Joe."

"The answer's no." He turned back to his beer.

She considered that, then took it in stride as merely the opening of negotiations. "One beer, please," she said, looking up at Stony's meteorite of a face. The beer materialized in front of her from Stony's plus-sized fist.

Joe stared at the frosted glass, willing it and the woman to go away. The determination he'd seen, and the desperation behind it, edged closer to the surface in those dark brown eyes. "I really do need your help. It's important."

"Still no."

That stopped her. Then a light dawned. "Oh, I'm ahead of myself. First things first, of course."

She danced the fingers of her right hand in the air over a small bump on the inside of her left wrist. Deep in Joe's pocket his wallet buzzed. Frowning, he glanced at it. Deposit registered, it said. A string of numbers hovered in the air above the tiny screen. He stared, blinked, and stared again. His account had grown an extra zero.

He scowled. "Well, that changes things."

The tension on her face eased towards relief. "Wonderful. You'll help me?"

He shook his head. "That changes my answer from no to a hard no. Get out of my bar."

She gazed at the drink in front of her, didn't touch it. She held her poise like the world-class diplomat he knew her to be. But the determination in those brown eyes faltered and the desperation flared. "I've looked everywhere, Joe. I really do need help. And it has to be you."

The beer in his own glass tasted sour. "Look lady," he said, "I don't know what's so important, but you could walk into a hundred other bars, anywhere in the Solar System, and find guys just like me sitting there. Go ask them."

"I need you to kill me, Joe. It's the most important thing there is. And you're the only one who can do it."

The silence in the bar was complete. Joe's simmering anger grew a touch of sympathy. "Not my business," he said, a little more softly. "Now if you'll excuse me."

"Will this help?" She waved her fingers again. Joe's wallet gave off a second buzz. He looked and raised an eyebrow.

Another zero.

"No, it wouldn't," he said.

"Oh." Her fingers moved again and her voice grew an edge. "Then how about this?"

Joe's wallet buzzed a third time. "Look, I don't care how much," he began, then he glanced. And stared. This time his account had a zero. Only a zero.

His anger and his reflexes acted without asking permission. The checkered, graphite pistol grip of his Sunfire 35 jumped into his hand and snapped a brilliant beam of yellow laser fire at a tiny, silver sphere he'd spotted hovering inside the door.

The sphere dodged and the beam flashed past, hitting the back wall of the bar with a sizzle. Chunks of scorching-hot moon rock hit the floor. A ragged hole in the wall let out a tendril of smoke as the woman's image flickered and stabilized.

"It won't be that easy. You'll have to find me first," she said. "But please hurry, there isn't much time."

She was gone. The tiny, silver holo generator fell to the barroom floor, dead. "Hologram," Joe muttered. A flood of embarrassment crowded out his irritation. It had been three years since his anger had gotten the better of him.

"Yah, we got that," rumbled Stony from the other side of the bar. "Never saw a portable one before. Speaking of which," he continued, nodding at the hole in the wall, "thought I told you not to use that thing in here. Next time I'm not gonna ask nice."

Joe's wallet buzzed once more. Deposit registered, it said again. His savings had reappeared, along with the original extra zero. A new memo said, 'for your expenses.' It was signed, Ella Pound.

He waved a finger and some of the extra cash flew over to Stony's account. The implant above Stony's left eye winked red. "Thanks," Stony growled, then waved at her beer. "She didn't drink that. Obviously. Help yourself."

Joe downed it in three long gulps, then lifted his butt off the stool. Unbidden and unwanted, Commander Garfield's voice rang through his head. 'When trouble takes a run at you, get off the launch pad. Can't do a thing if you're sitting still.'

Joe had spent three years trying to forget that voice. A long time, all things considered. But not nearly long enough.

As the door closed he heard the bar erupt into conversation.

Chapter 2

The door opened onto a plain, twenty-foot lava tube of ubiquitous grey Moon rock. Behind him, Joe knew, was the expanse of red lettering that proclaimed, Welcome to Stony's Bar and Grill – The Most Unfindable Bar in the Universe. A bit grandiose, since humanity had only just reached the Solar System's outer planets, but technically accurate. Before him was the thick, grey arch of the transpo booth, the size and shape of a door frame and filled with a haze of salt and pepper static.

The bar's entrance, the transpo booth, and that was it. The lava tube ended in smooth rock ten feet in either direction. Joe had looked, countless times, for the concealed stairway he'd hoped was there, but no dice. He stepped up to the booth, hating the cool sweat that had broken out on his forehead.

One Fare, Unlimited Distance, said his farecard. He tapped the coordinates for a remote, little-used booth and the static in the transpo frame coalesced into a dark grey and started to buzz. He dug a fist-sized rock out of his pocket and tossed it in.

The rock slipped into the wall of fuzz and disappeared. It didn't clang against the back wall of the cave. Instead, it went somewhere else.

An incomplete test, the bottom of his mind complained. It might be in space. It might be dust, or all the way to atoms, or on fire. No way to tell what's on the other side.

He'd developed a range of answers to the fear. Sometimes logic worked – particle transport was solid science, even if he didn't understand it. Sometimes calm explanation – millions of people all over the Solar System fuzzed around every day, and only a handful each year got rearranged. Occasionally he just bullied his feet into taking the next step.

Tonight, bothered and distracted by the woman's visit, he fell back on fatalism. One Fare, Unlimited Distance, his farecard said again. He reset the coordinates for a booth he knew, muttered, "Screw it," and stepped through.

Momentum, that was the key. A cold, electric thrill ran through his veins as the grey mist invaded his arm and leg, then wrapped around the rest of him, until he felt he was barely more coherent than the static itself. Kids were sent to dreamland with terrifying stories of what had happened to people who stopped in the static. The lucky ones, those who only hesitated, lost bits and pieces. Nobody ever found out what happened to those who stopped. But everyone knew. Joe's hindbrain knew.

He kept going and emerged from another booth on a side street in Heaviside City across town from his place. The neighborhood was quiet, deserted, most of the lights in the tidy apartment buildings off for the night. The city's circadian dome was set to transparent, letting the stars shine bright. He stood for a moment, wiggled his fingers and toes. All present and accounted for.

He never fuzzed into the booth in his neighborhood – a silly precaution, since few people knew him and even fewer wanted to find him, but old habits die hard. It was dark, hardly anybody around. A good night to think. He started walking.

Heaviside wore its layer of lunar dust like a sparkly mantle in the nighttime starlight. During the day, when the city's dome projected its holographic ball of light or real sunshine was allowed to pour through, the place looked as grubby as any town close to a mine, streets and buildings alike covered in the layer of gray, ashy dirt that passed for Moon soil. But at night the tiny flecks of crystals caught the starlight and set everything to twinkling. It was about as beautiful as the far side of the Moon ever got.

Joe trudged on through the night, not on alert, but surveying his surroundings with his usual automatic wariness. He'd chosen a transpo booth in the middle of the nightclub district, so his route took him through the heart of Heaviside. He sidestepped a group of partiers laughing their way home from a nearby club. He passed by the mouth of a dark alley and caught a glimpse of lumopaint graffiti on the side of the building, two raised fists breaking the shackles between them against a starry background shield. One fist was Mars-red, the other Earth-blue. Lowlifes Be Strong was scrawled underneath.

The occasional solitary soul hurried along with the purposeful gait of somewhere to be and not enough time to get there – nightshift workers, maybe, or someone late for bed. No sign of enforcement patrols, either on the street or in the air, but that didn't mean anything. Rebels were active in Heaviside. The patrols wouldn't be far away.

He caught the occasional glimpse of a deal going down in a side alley. Nothing that needed his special attention.

Dark-corners business was a feature of human society anywhere. He'd seen it on half a dozen worlds. Deals in Heaviside were visible if you looked, but they weren't out in broad daylight. The city had that much decorum and culture, at least.

These perimeter scans ran by reflex, occupying only a back corner of his brain. The rest of his head was full of one name.

Ella Pound. Joe knew her face. Everyone did. Ella was the only daughter of Wheeler Pound. Ella and her two older brothers were the heirs apparent to Pound Enterprises, which made them pretty much the richest off-Earth Elites in the Solar System.

The last family you'd ever expect to grace the doorstep of Stony's Bar and Grill.

When humanity had managed to slip the surly bonds of Earth and build colonies on the Moon, Wheeler's father Penfold supplied the prefabricated bases. When they reached Mars, Pound Industries had laid claim to vast tracts of the gritty Martian plains and found the coarse soil perfect for making synthcrete. The Pounds tapped into Mars' deep polar water reserves. Pound pavement covered the first rough roads, and later the city streets. Pound company prospectors lassoed the first asteroids, mining them for minerals to feed the depleted Earth. Back on the Moon, the anorthite and yttrium mines that employed much of Heaviside flew the Pound Enterprises flag.

So did every transpo booth in the Solar System. Pound Enterprises was stamped on the arched frame of each booth. When it all rolled together, one of every ten bucks spent off Earth passed through Wheeler Pound's thin, greedy hands.

Another night walker across the street gave Joe a half-wave. He returned the gesture, recognizing the man's face from earlier strolls. As much as he'd sought to be left to himself since arriving in Heaviside three years ago, Joe had become known in the community. Even respected around his own neighborhood. Unavoidable, probably. He trudged on through the higher buildings of the downtown core, keeping mostly to the shadows.

The celebrity holo lenses loved Ella. She was the public face of the family, a smart business decision when you considered her bulldog brothers and hawk-faced father. Ella had left the mining and construction concerns to them and siphoned some of the family fortune into a charitable concern. She spent her days championing the less fortunate in the name of Pound Enterprises. She attended the Elite balls and fundraisers, shook hands and gave speeches, all the while furthering the work of the Pound Endowment. She cut ribbons on community centers and libraries, doled out supplies to Lowlifes at food kitchens, consoled kids in their Pound Endowment hospital beds, while the holo lenses swooned.

Joe had never paid much attention. To the extent he'd thought about it, he figured she was doing her bit to improve the family reputation. Pound for Pound, that was the family motto.

Her appearance today was a damn puzzle. What the hell did she want with the likes of Joe Drive? And why the suicidal request? After three years of peace, he'd finally started to relax into a quiet, anonymous life. And now this.

The back corner of Joe's mind watched the character of the city change as he strode through it. The city made an effort to keep things clean and tidy in the downtown with regular sweepings and good patrols, and the city-center residents tried to keep things quiet after 10 o'clock at night. From the downtown, if you were looking for the recreation gyms and the music hall you went west. If you wanted nightlife you veered towards the rich districts of North Heaviside. If you were looking for art galleries and museums, you went to a city on the Nearside where the bright blue marble of Earth hung in the evening sky. But if you wanted none of those, if you craved a little place to live were the people were real and worked hard for a living, you headed towards Joe's neighborhood.

The Shaft, they called it. Joe had never quite figured out why. The Heaviside Crater mines were surface operations, no shafts involved. Maybe, he thought, it was a pithy comment on mining wages. Enough to live, barely, but never enough to leave. You moved to The Shaft when you felt like you'd fallen down a hole and were going to have a hell of a time climbing back out.

On the edge of The Shaft the alley business moved out into the open, people negotiating for their favorite panacea or weapon or companion on the street corners. More scrawls proclaiming things like Rebels Unite decorated the walls of buildings, sometimes accompanied by the badge of the rebels, the red fist and blue fist breaking a chain. Joe only bothered with the dealers or their customers when they forgot their civility and discretion, and ignored anything to do with the Resistance. He liked a bit of order in his neighborhood, that was all. In the three years since he'd moved in, The Shaft had discovered his preference and smoothed out its rough edges a little.

His attention grew more focused as he turned the last corner. His apartment building was fourth on the left, a pile of dark stone with cracked synthcrete steps up to the front door. The rest of the block was a mix of apartments and detached houses, all synthcrete and metal and in need of repair. This deep into the night, the block was quiet and orderly.

The second building from the corner was a single-floor prefab mining house, set almost flush with the sidewalk and ringed by an embarrassment of a white picket fence and a rusted gate. A young woman – he knew this only because he knew her, not from any physical distinguishing features on her skinny frame – creaked open the gate and called to him as he approached. She'd been waiting. "Joe, you gotta help me."

Get in line, he thought, but she didn't deserve an answer like that. "Evening, Dora," he said. "How are the kids?" That stopped her for a moment. Her eyes focused – a little hard for the left one, since it was blackened.

She said, "Cathy and Dawn? They're fine. They're over at my sister's place."

Joe nodded. "That's good. Is it Jumper again?"

Dora wrinkled up her nose. "Jumper? Nah, he's long gone. This is Ray. He's a mean one, Joe, and I didn't do nothing, promise."

"Huh." Joe had helped Dora out of a few fixes over the last year or two. Always to do with one or another of her boyfriends. They came and went like gnats on a warm summer night, but she always kept the kids out of it and he always gave her the same kind of help. "Where is he now?" he asked.

"Home." She gestured over her shoulder at the house. Every window was dark.

"So he just swung at you, out of the blue, did he?"

"Well," said Dora, and left it at that. Joe knew the story by now. Dora was maybe a bit of a handful, and she tended to choose men with limited capacity for patience. But still. He looked at her eye. It was fresh, swelling more as he watched. That wasn't okay.

"You know, you could leave him. Kick him out," Joe offered.

"Well, yeah, thing is he's got a job."

"Hmm," said Joe. "I'll see what I can do. You take care

of yourself, Dora."

"You too, Joe. Thanks."

The steps up to his apartment building were gritty but swept clean of trash. He let himself through the front door and then into his apartment. The door closed with a soft whoosh and a series of half a dozen clicks.

"Lights," he said, "air." The lights came on and a soft breeze wafted away the last of the stink from the dark, dilapidated hallway outside. The fireplace against the far wall whumped into life. From the street, he knew, his windows still appeared dark.

He'd managed to carve out a nice place in the middle of The Shaft. He owned this apartment, the one above and the one below, had connected them all and reinforced the entire group. Then he'd made it simple but comfortable. The interior of this floor resembled a mountain cabin, with homey paintings and a stuffed pheasant, solid, comfortable furniture and a make-believe fireplace that crackled in the far wall. The kitchen, off to the side, held Earth-quality fixtures next to barnwood cupboards.

No one in the neighborhood had seen the inside of Joe's place. They wouldn't understand.

The renovations had taken much of his accumulated savings and the lump sum resettlement amount, standard issue for soldiers who pensioned out of the Interstellar Space Force. Now he got by on the monthly allotment and a few odd bucks that he'd tucked away for a rainy day. Which made Ella Pound's offer, to his irritation, hard to refuse. There had been a rainy day or two in the past couple of years. As much as he hated to admit it, Joe's money was getting short.

Ella Pound had given his savings a good bump. He could take it and do nothing. Forget he'd ever seen her. Forget her ridiculous demand. Forget all the extra zeros she'd promised.

It would be tough, but he could.

What wasn't so forgettable was how easily she'd done it. She had found him. Called him by name. With the flick of a finger she'd placed scads of money into his personal account, then emptied it with another. She'd walked through three years of careful privacy like it was the thinnest of veils. The ease of it had shocked him. The Elite arrogance of it had angered him.

Sleep wasn't going to come tonight, not yet. He rolled the mess around in his head for another ten minutes and got nowhere. Ella Pound's visit simply made no sense whatever. He needed more information, if it was out there to be found.

He needed to go downstairs.

The fireplace, nestled inside its solid slate mantelpiece, let off a steady, soothing warmth. On top of the mantelpiece was a miniature grandfather clock, an old fashioned revolver and a picture of his mother on their old Idaho acreage. The clock had the look of a wind up affair, with actual hands that spun around and pointed to actual numbers on the face. He flipped open the glass cover, stuck out his index finger and twiddled the hour hand three times around the dial, letting it rest exactly on eight o'clock.

Nothing happened. He closed the clock's glass, then strode forward through the fireplace. The heat from the fire grew hot, then hotter, then a moment of very hot that washed over him with the thickness of paper as he stepped through the hologram and into a plain stairwell. Fourteen steps down he pressed a red button on the wall and stepped out into the basement apartment.

This one had the same layout as the main floor. The décor was a little different. Instead of country cabin, this room was a cross between end-of-the-universe bunker and Interstellar Space Force intelligence hub.

The kitchen was stacked with enough provisions to last him through a three month siege. The living room held weapon and ammunition crates, most with the ISF logo still etched on their sides. The dining room featured a console and holo rig that he'd liberated from a Space Force ops base just moments before a rebel attack had melted the building to slag. His former employers had no idea it still existed.

The contents of the basement apartment could have him sent to prison on Ganymede, if anyone ever found out about it.

Joe looked about the place, saw the fine layer of dust on most of the crates, and sighed. He'd hardened and stocked this apartment because he was a soldier, and knew that fortune and continued life favored the prepared. Still, he'd hoped never to need it. Now he strode to the console, flipped on the power and slotted in an anonymizer.

"Ella Pound." He said it out loud as he sent out the search string. Naming the demon, he supposed. But was she? Not very many demons wanted you to end them. Came right out, in fact, and said it had to be you.

In a moment his screens flooded with information.

He cruised through all the basic family biography everybody knew. He slowed and dug deeper when he came to Ella's charitable work. Joe had always assumed that Wheeler Pound had sliced a few credits off the family fortune to keep his daughter busy and pay for some public relations. In fact, he saw, Ella had browbeat the money out of her dad. She'd leveraged the funds into more donations from across the Solar System's Elites and used the proceeds to help the less fortunate.

He scanned her personal life. No husband, no kids, no significant others ever, as far as he could tell. No one but the family and the Endowment in her life. Wasn't that a sad state of affairs? Ella belonged to no social clubs, no groups apart from her own philanthropic endeavor. She had no apparent hobbies. She did no public travel.

Of course not. The Pounds had their own fleet of spacejets. The web was jammed with pictures of Ella at society functions all over the Solar System, surrounded by the cream of the Elites. In his professional estimation she outshone them all. Other images showed her shaking hands with dignitaries, accepting donations, feeding kids in soup lines, opening hospital wings. There was even one photo of Ella Pound bringing Endowment blankets to the wounded during the Aphrodite Colony Uprising near the south pole of Venus.

Joe checked the date of the photo and hmphed into the silence of his bunker. She'd been there three days before his bombing run had surgically removed the three leaders, effectively stopping the Uprising in its tracks.

He spent another hour rolling through the mountain of data on Ella Pound that told him precious little about the woman herself. The only curious detail, mentioned at the bottom of a recent news story, was that Ella was currently enjoying a quiet retreat time on Poundville, the family asteroid in orbit around Mars.

There was no sign of suicidal tendencies. No hint of trouble of any kind. At the end of the hour he still had no idea what the hell she was up to.

"Forget it," he said to the room. So she knew who he was and how to find him. It had only been a matter of time, anyway. So she could reach into his accounts at will, add and subtract as she pleased. That irked him a lot more. But in the end, the defining fact of his life remained. He wanted to be left alone.

"Forget it," he said again. He put his tech to sleep and went upstairs to do the same.

Chapter 3

In the morning Joe picked through his kitchen, didn't like what he saw, and decided on breakfast at Stony's. He locked up his apartment and stepped out to greet the new Lunar day.

The back side of the Moon was halfway through its natural two-week night, so the Circadian dome blazed with a warm, holographic sun rising in a sapphire blue sky. The Lunar climate planners had learned a few lessons about artificial weather over the past 50 years. Once the Peter Foundation had boosted the Moon's gravity to Earth-normal and a decent atmosphere was established, the colony had grown fast with transplants from the home planet. On a terraformed celestial body the weather was whatever you made it. But human beings came with millennia of habituation to an actual planet, so they needed variety. Six days out of the week were the standard, predictable mix of sunshine or rain under the city domes, planned months in advance. The seventh day had come to be known as dice day. The climate planners literally rolled a pair of dice to decide what the weather was going to be.

Today was dice day, and Joe stepped out into a brilliantly warm and sunny morning with an absurd amount of dew glistening on every surface. "Pretty," he muttered to himself, threw his jacket over his arm and kept on going.

The streets of The Shaft were quiet, in the hour of hang time between the departure of workers for the mines and the emergence of those left at home. Joe turned south to find a transpo booth. Then he remembered his promise of the night before, sighed and headed up the block.

He ignored the entry plate and knocked on the door of the little house. After a minute Dora opened the door, swung it wide when she saw who was there, and stepped aside to let Joe pass. "Thank you," she mouthed as he walked into the gloom.

Prefab houses from Pound Enterprises were quick, easy and identical, an ideal solution for corporate housing. They all smelled of synthcrete and held on to a tenacious, dank humidity. Dora hadn't yet blanked the windows or aired the place out for the day. Joe found Ray by the smell of breakfast coming from the kitchen.

Which seemed to consist of a stack of micro waffles and the first of the day's beer, judging from what was on the kitchen table. Ray himself sat in a chair in his underwear, thick body showing remnants of his muscular youth but already overlaid with the pallid skin and layer of fat that was going to dominate the rest of his life. Ray had blonde hair buzzed short, the ubiquitous miner's cut. The better to wash out the grit.

"Who the fuck?" he started, beginning to rise as Joe came into the room. Joe waved him back down and grabbed the chair across the table.

"No problem, only here for a moment. Keep eating," Joe said. Ray didn't look pleased but he did look caught at a disadvantage. Warily he sat back down. He left the micro waffles alone and grabbed the beer more like a weapon than a drink. "Now, here's the thing," Joe said, "and believe me this isn't the first time Dora and I have had this conversation. I really don't know where she finds you guys, but she seems to have some kind of a fatal attraction to all the wrong types. You know the types I'm talking about?" Joe continued, pointedly ignoring the whitening fingers on the neck of Ray's beer. "The kind who don't know how to treat a lady right."

"Oh, really?" Ray spoke up. He had the gravelly voice of a long-time mine rat. The steady job Dora had mentioned. "Is that what she told you?"

"That's what her eye told me."

Ray had the good grace to look a bit embarrassed. "Yeah. Well. She got on my nerves, is all."

Joe sighed again. He wanted to wrap this up fast. The smell of Ray's meal was killing his appetite. "That can happen sometimes. I'm sure it goes the other way, too, right?"

The fingers on the bottle whitened again. "Fuck you are, coming into my house and telling me all this? Find the door before I dust you." Ray shoved his chair back, but didn't get to his feet.

Joe felt the tingle at the base of his spine but kept his hands still. "Hey, it's early in the morning, I caught you off guard, I get that. There's no problem here. Tell you what. I'll ask the only question that counts and then I'll get out." He burrowed a gaze into Ray's eyes. "Do you love her? Hell, maybe that's a lot. Do you respect her?"

Ray's eyes were droopy with leftover sleep, red from constant exposure to Moon dust, and hazel. The beer had given them a bit of a shine. As Joe watched the question strike home, they shifted. A momentary flicker to the side before they came back hard. "The hell? What the hell kind of question is that?" He shifted his grip on the beer bottle and lifted it off the table.

All the answer Joe needed. He sighed once more and let the tingle take over.

Ray was pretty fast for an overbuilt miner with undeveloped fine motor skills. Joe rose from the table at the same speed as Ray, lifted his left arm to match Ray's swing. His forearm caught the bottle mid-flight. Glass shards filled the air, continuing towards Joe's face like tiny spears, but he was on the move and no longer there. His right hand flicked out and snatched a waffle as he rotated forward across the table.

Ray was already off balance, his right arm swept wide by Joe's block and his foot caught under his falling chair. When Joe's hand crammed the waffle into his open mouth and kept on going, Ray's momentum accelerated into the kitchen wall. The back of his head dented the foam insulation over the synthcrete and he went down, spluttering and gagging crumbs all over his undershirt.

Joe checked his left arm – a tiny nick from the glass – and swung down to grab the front of Ray's undershirt. He hoisted the guy back onto his feet. Ray's nose was bleeding, making a mess everywhere. "Time for you to leave, don't you think?" Ray thought, then nodded. "And not come back, and not bother Dora again. You two are done, right?" Another nod. "And your place," Joe continued. "It's not in The Shaft, is it?"

Ray went to burble a complaint, then he looked at Joe's face. Saw something that changed his mind. He shook his head.

"Good. I have to go now, but I trust you. You'll be dressed and gone in two minutes and never come back. I won't see you around, Ray." He dropped the boy into his chair, wiped a spot of blood off his wrist with a cloth from the sink, and left.

Dora was waiting for him at the front door. "Did you

have to?" she whined, looking miserable. "He's got a job."

"He's not worth it, Dora," Joe muttered. "Say, I've had a bit of luck lately. I'll send you a little something to tide you over."

"Tide me over to what?" she said. "Tide's out, Joe. It's out."

He had no answer for that.

Chapter 4

The Peter Foundation didn't believe in pampering its acolytes with creature comforts, but they sure laid on the ceremony. Ryza stood in the quiet of his tiny lavatory and tied the complex knot that held the red sash of his good ceremonial cloak, looking in the mirror to make sure he got it right. Over his shoulder in the mirror was the door to his small, silent living quarters, deep in the heart of the Foundation's quiet dormitories.

Sometimes it was so quiet around this place he felt like screaming just to hear the noise.

He gave the mirror a final check. The ceremonial cloak was pure white, without blemish. The red sash of the Engineers identified his department, the two gold stripes at its end his position as Senior Analyst. He'd trimmed his half inch of ash-blond hair and cleaned his teeth. Everything was in order for his report to the Council.

Which was important, because they weren't going to like it.

He stepped out into the achingly bright sunshine of the mountains outside Nazca, Peru and strode across the Peter Foundation's sprawling campus to the Pyramid. The central shrine sat in the middle of the tan desert clay, its four sides of sloping obsidian rising to a single point capped with white. The Council building had filled him with awe when he'd first been invited to join the Foundation. Today he just squinted against the glare that bounced off the polished slab.

The guards outside the Council chamber doors had shared a drink with him in the pub last night, but there was no conversation between them now. Not here. They bowed, gestured a welcome with their hands and pulled open the heavy bronze doors, waving him through.

So much ceremony, he thought to himself. So much mystery and mumbo jumbo for an organization founded on science. He stepped through into the bright and airy chamber, its ceiling the white, translucent capstone on top of the building.

The seven Sages of the Council faced him across their crescent rostrum, waiting for him to take his place in the sunken oval before them. He placed the slim folder holding his report on the lectern in the center of the oval and bowed to Uchenna, the Chairman. Uchenna returned the bow with a small bend of his waist. The wrinkles of his midnight-colored face arranged themselves into a polite smile.

You're moving slowly today, thought Ryza. The anti-aging treatments must be failing you.

"Engineer Ryza, Senior Analyst of the Peter Foundation, you have been away from the home planet, observing. Now you have come to report. We welcome you."

"Chairman Uchenna, honored Sages, I have been watching and now I am home. Here is my report." The silly ritual over, Ryza took a breath and added, "It's not good out there, sir."

Uchenna leaned forward in his chair and warmed into a fatherly smile. "It is good to have you back, Ryza. When we granted you Senior Analyst status and gave you the freedom to travel and observe where you wished, I knew you would take advantage of it. Now we get to reap the rewards of your journeys. Take your time. Tell us what you've seen."

Ryza didn't want to take his time. He wanted the leaders of the Peter Foundation to do something. "The imbalance in the Solar System increases with each passing day, Sages. I've watched the mines and factories on the Moon, Mars and Venus get larger, suck in more workers and treat them very poorly. I've sat in taverns and markets and listened to the workers' complaints. I know the lives they lead in the Lowlife villages and towns. I've also wandered through the cities, sat in the uptown markets and cafes, observed the lives of those who run the industries. I'll say it again, Chairman, it's not good. The Lowlifes are worked hard and have almost nothing to show for it. The Elites rule with an iron hand and live in luxury. They give no advantages to the workers and are harsh with any dissent.

"I've seen more signs of the Resistance. The Lowlifes are trying to fight for a better life, to organize into an effective voice. But the Elites have enlisted the help of the Interstellar Space Force somehow, even though the ISF is directed by the Home Alliance here on Earth. The fighting, where it breaks out, is brutal. The rebels had the upper hand for a time, but now they are losing again, and badly."

Uchenna and the rest of the Council sat in their elevated seats and listened. Uchenna's smile had dropped away. When a moment had passed in silence he asked, "Thank you for your report. We will add it to the Algorithm's information sources. Do you have anything else to add?"

He'd sweated over this moment. As a junior project engineer his job had been to tend the Foundation's graviton modulators on the Moon, Mars and elsewhere. He'd also spent time in the Foundation labs developing useful items that humanity might need. That was the Peter Foundation's job, as far as he saw it, to help humanity prosper and grow. His job had never been to speak his mind to the Council.

But now he was a Senior Analyst. His job had changed. He took another deep breath and rose to his position.

"We have to do something, Chairman. What does the Algorithm say? People all across the Solar System are under stress and it's only a matter of time before something breaks. We're supposed to guide humanity, aren't we? I think some guidance is needed right now. What does the Algorithm say about all of this? What does Peter say, for that matter?"

A quiet murmur went around the crescent table, almost silent, little more than an intake of breath. Now I've done it, Ryza thought.

Uchenna was long past smiling. "Senior Analyst Ryza, your rank gives you the privilege to voice your opinions. We welcome them, and thank you for being so frank with us. But I think you forget how the Peter Foundation works. We observe. We calculate possible futures for humanity with the help of the Algorithm, and the Prognosticator that interprets it. When we see an action that needs to be taken to correct humanity's course, we intervene. We invent what is needed, nudge where required, help when necessary. But we also understand the consequences of rash, unplanned action. Peter has taught us this. He created the Algorithm to help guide our decisions. And he instilled in us the most important philosophy of all: Make no move before its time. Observe and report, until the right action at the right time becomes clear."

Uchenna leaned forward in his chair. His face, although firm, wasn't forbidding. "We are open to suggestions, Ryza. What action do you propose we take?"

He gave the only answer he had. "I don't know. But

something, surely. Things are getting bad, Council. We must be able to do something."

Uchenna nodded. "The Algorithm agrees with you on that one point, Senior Analyst. The right action and the right time are not yet clear. So we continue to watch and report. However," he added, "I can assuage your impulsive nature. A – concern – has arisen. The Algorithm has given us the name of a man. He will be given a task. He will come into possession of an object."

Ryza waited for more. Uchenna had that ghost of a smile back on his face, a slim line of white teeth showing against his dark face. Finally Ryza asked, "Is that all? A concern, a task, and an object?"

Now Uchenna broke into a full smile. "You begin to see the nature of our work. The Algorithm, and the Prognosticator machine that interprets it, are parsimonious with specifics. Often we have to do our best with what we get. But we do know this. The man is reluctant to act. However, he must undertake the mission he is given. He stands at a pivot point in the flow of events, and his involvement is crucial. He needs, shall we say, a bit of a nudge. I can think of no one better suited to the job."

The folder containing Ryza's report slipped into the lectern, and a new one took its place. Ryza picked it up, excited at the prospect of doing something. He paused before taking his leave. "What does the Algorithm say about the object?"

Uchenna's smile left. "It gives us silence. I, myself, have queried the Prognosticator every way that I can. It may be nothing. Or something. I leave that for you to discover and report. Happy journey, Senior Analyst Ryza."

Chapter 5

The walk to the transpo booth, despite the sunny warmth, added to the tiny knot of trouble in Joe's mind. 'The tide's out, Joe. It's out.' Dora's parting words stayed with him and forced him to look around.

The Shaft almost looked beautiful in the morning light. Windows glinted, tenements and houses appeared a bit less shabby. He saw a few people sweeping their stairs and walks, doing endless battle against the lunar dust. He even heard a shopkeeper hum a tune as he opened up his stall.

But underneath it all was grime and despair. He'd never seen it this clearly. Maybe he hadn't wanted to. The people of The Shaft – off-duty miners, business owners, young mothers out with their kids – looked worse-off than he remembered. More patches on their clothes. A slower pace, as if they had nowhere in particular to go and no one was waiting for them at the other end. Drawn expressions under the appreciation of the day, a deep desperation that they all shared.

Another rebel shield had been lumopainted onto a corporate building, this one a Pound Transport local office. On the front of the building, bold as brass. The red fist and blue fist duking it out against the stars was so fresh the paint still glistened.

A squad of Interstellar Space Force grunts was busy scrubbing it off. Joe shook his head as he passed by on the other side of the street. That was no work for an ISF soldier. Maybe they'd torn up a club and this was their punishment.

He scowled as he got closer to the transpo booth, wishing for the hundredth time that Stony wasn't so particular about how his patrons got to the bar. This one was on a main street corner and had a few people in line. He joined them and watched. A young woman went through carrying a baby in her arms, disappearing into the mist without a thought. Next went a businessman, so focused on his link that he barely looked up to make sure he'd entered the right coordinates. The grey, man-tall frame filled with smoky static, the guy strode into it and was gone.

Right in front of Joe was a kid, maybe seventeen, with a duffel in one hand and a sheaf of papers in the other, leaning forward on the balls of his feet with eagerness. Glancing over the kid's shoulder, Joe recognized the paperwork. Interstellar Space Force recruitment papers. The same bleak pallor as everyone else lined the boy's face, but lightened by a new hope. He'd found his way out of The Shaft.

Don't get your hopes up, kid, Joe wanted to say. Don't believe everything they tell you. But he held his silence as the boy punched in the coordinates for the recruitment center and marched into the fuzz.

No screams. No howls of horror or dismay from the other side of the booth as people arrived on the other side minus a body part. But then, there wouldn't be, would there?

Man up, he growled to himself. Several people now stood behind him, waiting their turn. Joe ran the informal mantra of the transpo booth through his head – those who hesitate are lost – waved Stony's business card at the booth to input the secret coordinates, waved his farecard at the machine to power it up, held his breath and sped into the grey fuzz.

He stepped out into the lava tube outside the bar. The cave looked as drab and featureless as it always did, lit by the red glow from the lettering announcing Stony's Bar. Joe counted appendages, then checked his farecard. One Fare, Unlimited Distance, it read. He gave it an affectionate flick. As much as he hated transpo booths, he knew he'd miss this card when it died.

The card had been a gift from a tech guy who worked for Pound Enterprises and knew a few loopholes in the system, a thank-you for Joe's help getting out of a jam. The card was a ghost. Transpo booths could send you anywhere up to half a planet away, if you had the credit. Joe's was always primed for one trip, unlimited distance. The moment he used it, two things happened. The balance reset. And all record of his trip was wiped from Pound Enterprises' corporate memory.

"It'll be good forever!" his friend had announced. "Or until they find out about it." So far, so good.

The place was mostly empty. Breakfast smells hung in the air from the kitchen behind the bar. Stony had the bar lined with glasses and was picking them up one at a time, holding them in three fingers of his massive right paw while polishing them with a fresh rag. "Morning," Joe called out. Stony nodded.

Joe glanced over at the wall that he had perforated the day before. Good as new. He couldn't even see the scorch marks. "I just repaired that," Stony growled.

"Thank the girl. It's her money I paid you with."

Stony considered this. "So you're gonna do it, then."

"Do what? Do that?" Joe was incredulous. "You've got to

be kidding. Whatever gave you that idea?"

Stony squinted at him with one eye. "Contract law. You take the money, you do the job."

Joe hadn't thought of it like that. He refused to think about it like that now. He shook his head as he found a seat. "Can't make a contract with an insane person. She practically forced that money down my throat, put it directly into my account. I consider it payment for the irritation."

Stony rolled that over in his mind for a second. "Works for me," he said.

The door to the kitchen whooshed open as Stony's daughter Everest swung through it, long, brown hair flying and breakfast plates in hand. She was doing Old West Retro today, Joe saw, with skin-tight blue work pants below and green-checked gingham shirt above, complete with lace at the cuffs. Joe watched as she hustled the plates over to a far table, sat them down and engaged the patrons in friendly conversation.

Everest was by far – until yesterday – the most beautiful person ever to grace Stony's Bar and Grill. She was also, being Stony's daughter, totally off limits to the male clientele. Not that any of them would push their luck. At five-nine, amply proportioned, with a bustline that deserved her name, Everest was perfectly capable of taking care of herself. Joe figured he'd have about a sixty-forty chance of survival were he ever drunk enough to try an advance without being invited.

"Hey," Joe said, when Everest appeared at his table.

"Hey yourself, Drive. Don't often see you in here for breakfast. What'll you have?"Joe ordered the special and a cup of coffee. "You got it." She headed back into the kitchen.

Joe scanned the bar. Brown wood beams made a show of holding up the whitewashed stone walls and paneled ceiling, even though the whole establishment had been carved out of solid rock. Air conditioning hummed through the vents, but the place always smelled the same, a rich and somehow pleasing mix of whiskey, wood polish, home cooking and Moon rock. A few regulars dotted the tables. None of them were near the back with Joe.

The bar had come to feel almost like his second home. He'd first stumbled into Stony's a few months after landing in Heaviside, still feeling untethered, cut loose from the military by his own design and unsure of what came next. He'd struck up a conversation with a stranger on a sightseeing trip to the crater, and when they'd parted the man handed him a Stony's Bar business card.

Stony and Everest served up beer and laughter, and Joe eventually became a good friend. In the deep shelter of this welcoming place he'd buried his former life, built a new one. Over the last three years he'd begun the long process of forgetting what he'd done.

Until yesterday. Until Ella Pound had found him and brought it all back.

"Well, screw you," muttered Joe to the memory of Ella Pound's hologram sitting beside him.

"Pardon?" said Everest, setting down his breakfast.

"I didn't mean you," said Joe, "sorry."

"I should hope not. That's a lousy invitation. I'm certain you can do better." Joe let out a chuckle. He also felt his face heat up around the cheekbones. Laughing at him, Everest headed away towards the bar.

The bacon was from terraformed farmland in Tycho Crater, the eggs from a coop at the edge of the Heaviside dome. The coffee, however, was genuine Earthside, and how Stony acquired it Joe had no clue. The aroma alone perked up his day.

Halfway through the first cup Joe felt the air pressure in the place quiver. Someone had just opened the door and closed it again. He glanced up.

He'd never seen the guy in here before, that was for sure. The newcomer was tall, laser beam skinny. He needed a barber. On the far side of middle age, he had the look that men get when they've done too many shifts in the mines - owlish and staring, like they don't quite remember what the outside world looks like.

Joe bent back to his breakfast, then up again. The skinny guy still hadn't come down the three steps. He was scanning the place, trying to look like he wasn't.

Somewhere deep in his mind, Joe's training woke up. Trouble had just come through the door. He knew what would happen next, so he bent down to his plate and shoveled in a few more mouthfuls of Everest's cooking. Too good to let it go to waste.

On the third spoonful, right on cue, Joe saw the new arrival slide onto the chair opposite his. "You're Joe Drive," said a thin, dusty voice. Definitely a miner.

"So I've been told. Break orbit and burn, guy." The old warning came easily to his lips.

"Wow. Hey, heard you had a visitor yesterday," the guy continued. Joe said nothing and managed another mouthful. "Heard she said some pretty crazy stuff." Joe gave him silence. "Just wanted to let you know that's exactly what it was. Crazy. You shouldn't think about doing anything about it. No, not a thing. Because that'd be crazy, too."

Joe gave the coffee all the attention it deserved.

"So that was all crazy, right? Not anything you'll do anything about, right?"

Joe hovered his fork over the plate, considering one more bite. Then the plate, with half his breakfast still on it, slid over to the other side of the table. He glimpsed a laser tattoo on the man's arm. A red fist shackled to a blue fist. The seedy guy bent down, stuck his beak of a nose directly in Joe's line of sight with a remarkable lack of self preservation, and repeated the question. "Right?"

Don't do it, Joe told himself. Still, there was the fork and there was the guy's nose. And this was the second irritation in as many days. He sighed again and decided to resist the urge. "Listen. What I decide to do or not is my own business. What I'm deciding to do right now," he pulled the plate back, "is finish my breakfast. Once more, friend, break orbit and burn."

A sheen of sweat broke out on the guy's brow.

'Don't even think it,' Joe almost said, but the poor sod was already swinging a wide roundhouse with his right, coming up from underneath the table with a sock full of ball bearings in his hand. Joe let the sock go through three quarters of an arc and then lifted his left hand, contacted the guy's upper arm and changed the geometry of his swing. The business end of the makeshift sap altered course, swung inwards and caught the fellow square on his beak of a nose.

The skinny miner flipped backwards out of his chair, the back of his head hitting the floor with a resounding thud.

Joe picked up the fork from where he'd placed it, reclaimed his plate and grabbed another bite.

The guy collected his wits a moment later, fingered his nose. Bruised and bleeding but not broken. He looked up at Joe sheepishly. "Worth a try," he mumbled. Joe gestured towards the chair. The guy righted it and sat down again.

"Who made it worth a try?" Joe asked.

"Tall fella," said the seedy guy. "Elite, from the look of him. Didn't belong there, that's for damn sure. Said he had a job for me, something that needed doing but he didn't have the time himself. I says, how bad you want it done? He flicked his fingers, like that," the guy demonstrated, "and bam! My account had an extra zero in it."

"Hmm," Joe countered. "Enough for you to forget your values." He gestured at the Lowlifes Resist tattoo on the guy's wrist.

"For one job? Yeah, it was."

"And I was the job?" Joe pressed.

He nodded. "All I had to do was convince you that whatever you heard yesterday was stupid. And make absolutely sure you weren't going to do anything about it."

Well, shit. Joe mulled over this latest bit of news and didn't like it. Not at all. He noted the sock still hanging limp in the guy's hand. "And that?"

"Oh." Even more sheepishly, the guy tucked it away. "If it still looked like you were going to do something about it," he shrugged, "I was to make sure you couldn't."

Joe nodded. "Listen," he said, "you have any idea who I talked to yesterday, or what they said that I'm not supposed to do anything about?"

The skinny guy shook his head. "Nope. Not a clue."

"Good," said Joe. "Keep it that way. You're gonna see that guy again?" The miner nodded. "Tell him whatever you want to. Tell him I agreed. Tell him you knocked me silly. Whatever. Just get out of here and don't ever let me see you again." The guy rose to go and Joe stopped him. "Hey, wait. How did you get here?"

"Oh." The guy reached into a pocket and pulled out a Stony's Bar coordinates card. "Guy handed me this. Told me where you'd be. Told me when. Seemed to know everything about you."

"Wonderful." Joe snatched the card away. "Now get gone."

The miner rose and slunk for the door, avoiding eye contact with the others in the bar. At the middle step he turned back. "The dude in black said he'd give me an extra zero to make sure."

And there was the gun. A Sneaky Pete, a low-wattage laser built for concealment. Not much more than a pencil-thin tube with a trigger button, it emitted a needle beam that couldn't penetrate walls but, at close range, could go through a human just fine.

Before the guy raised his weapon another inch Joe's mind had run the calculus. He knew two things to a reasonable certainty.

First was the method of attack. The seedy guy wasn't going to aim, just press the button and draw a broad, blazing sweep across the room. Which would slice up Joe's table, Joe's breakfast and Joe.

Second was that, even though the Sunfire was already in his hand and rising above the table, he wouldn't be fast enough.

I've gotten slow, he chastised himself. Rusty. I wonder what it'll feel like. Probably hot as hell.

A roar of superheated air blasted through the room. A brilliant, white flash pixellated the world into dots in front of Joe's eyes. The smells of ozone and bad barbecue filled the bar. Didn't know a Sneaky Pete had that much punch, Joe thought. And it didn't even hurt.

In fact, he was nose-down on the floor and still in one piece. People were screaming out there somewhere. The air scrubber ran itself up to a high whine, sucking the smoke out of the bar. He hauled himself back onto his chair.

Everest stood by the kitchen door and shoved a long, black tube, its business end squashed into a thick wedge, back underneath the bar.

He looked over to where the old miner had stood. Lying on the floor was the Sneaky Pete and half a hand. One finger still rested on the button. A black streak ran partway up the wall behind the steps.

A Sneaky Pete was a precise, minimalist tool. Just enough power to win the argument. An Eraser, on the other hand, was built to stop the argument in its tracks. And make sure there was never another one. Its eight yttrium-coated lenses sent out an overstrength wall of destruction powerful enough to vaporize a polar bear. That one shot had raised the temperature in the bar ten degrees.

Stony still polished the glasses. Everest, a sour look on her face, began to dig around in a closet for a bucket and a mop. Joe got up and went over to help. It was the least he could do.

"You know that thing's illegal," he muttered under his breath."I haven't even seen an Eraser in years."

"Why drill a hole through a guy when you can make him disappear?" Everest said back. "Like we tell people, Stony's Bar and Grill is a safe place. Once you're here, nobody bothers you." She looked up from filling the bucket, a hard gleam in her eye. "Nobody."

"Ain't that the truth," Stony said. "Still," he continued, "appears like you're a bit of a hot rock there, Joe. I'm gonna have to ask you to bow out for a while." He stuck out his hand.

"Really?" Joe asked. Stony nodded. Feeling like he'd just been exiled, Joe handed over both cards, his and the one he'd taken from the uninvited guest.

He helped Everest mop up the mess, then he left. Outside the door, before he convinced himself to go back into the transporter, he turned for a last look. Without a coordinates card, how would he ever find Stony's again?

He fuzzed back home, his mind embroiled in a slow burn. This business had cost him his sanctuary.

Chapter 6

The transpo gave an extra crackle as Joe used it to beam himself, not back home, but to a lonely transporter station on a bluff overlooking the Number 3 Mine at the north edge of Heaviside Crater. He'd never been able to figure out why someone had thought this a good place to plant a transpo booth, but he wasn't complaining. The view was a Lunar version of pretty.

The rim of the crater arched from horizon to horizon before him, its peaks and crags eroded smooth after 4 billion years, swooping down to a flat opening at the northernmost edge. Heaviside City was visible through the gap. The city dome extended out over this part of the crater – not the whole of Heaviside Crater, which was a hundred miles across, but enough to cover the Number 3 Mine. The bluff where he stood rose 3000 feet straight up from the crater floor, then swooped down behind him in a long, lazy meadow covered with tough Moon grass.

Gravity was a touch lighter at this altitude, the air thin and clear. The Peter Foundation had installed their first gravity device on the Moon, and it was serviceable enough, delivering Earth-normal gravity at the surface and enough pull to hold on to an atmosphere. Joe had only a vague notion of how it all worked. Something to do with a chunk of superdense space rock, and a fiendishly complex instrument at the Moon's south pole that fine-tuned gravity wherever they wanted it. Nobody outside the Peter Foundation had ever even seen the thing. Foundation Devices were the best-guarded installations in the Solar System.

Once the new gravity had been established on the Moon, terraformers and settlement builders had gone to work. Now, 40 years later, the results were evident, even here in the middle of nowhere. The planned rain cycle in this sector a couple of days ago had freshened up the tough, blueish grass on the meadow until it was almost green.

Joe hung his legs over the edge of the ridge to watch the crawlers and diggers scratch out the minerals far beneath, and fumed.

He'd had three years of a nice, quiet life. It had been three years since he'd mashed Commander Garfield's face to a pulp in the officer's mess for his betrayal, thrown down his crossed thrusters and resigned from the Interstellar Space Force. Ever since, Joe had kept his silence. Not said a word to anyone about what they had made him do. In return, Garfield had put him on indefinite leave and approved a pension, even though they both knew he was never coming back. They'd left each other alone.

Joe had carved out a life here in Heaviside, away from everything, minding his own business. He'd been – happy? Maybe not. But he'd been invisible.

Now one visit from some deranged Elite had brought home a threat on his life and barred him from the only refuge he'd found. He was irritated. He wanted to shoot something. But he wasn't angry enough to grant Ella Pound's insane wish.

Gradually the light faded. The crawlers and diggers a half-mile below him eased to a stop. The workers had all fuzzed back to Heaviside by the time Joe brushed the grass off his butt and went home to bed.

He awoke in the dark of midnight with the Sunfire 35 laser pistol in his hand and his heart racing. Ella Pound stood in his bedroom, bright as day, slightly larger than she'd been in the bar. Her long hair was down and a little tousled. She sported mauve parasilk pajamas so sheer that wherever they touched her he could practically feel the curve. Not going there, he told himself.

Out loud he said, "What the hell, lady."

She was looking around, fiddling with something beyond the edge of the hologram. She tossed a glance over her shoulder. "I don't have much time," she said, distracted. "They're always listening, always monitoring. It's the middle of the night here and I'm not sure – " she paused, noticing him for the first time. "Oh! Is it the middle of the night for you, too?"

"You accessed the hologram generators in my bedroom. What did you expect?"

She walked over and sat down beside him on the edge of the mattress. The only way he could tell she wasn't actually with him was that the mattress wasn't dented. "Have you decided? Will you help?" She stared into him with those mahogany brown eyes.

"Help?" he answered. "Help with what? For you to commit suicide? Look, Ms. Pound, you're probably new to this, but there are a hundred ways to take care of that yourself. And if it has to be by someone else, there are about a million other people you could have chosen besides me."

She shook her head. "No, I'm constantly watched. It has to be you. You're the only one with – " her image flickered and faded. She reached out again beyond the screen and the image stabilized. "I don't have much time."

"You know, you got me in trouble already," Joe complained. "Somebody came to Stony's Bar this morning to kill me."

Ella's face paled in shock, an effect that spoke to the quality of the hologram. "I'm sorry, Joe," she said. "They're on to you. I had no idea they would move so fast. You've got to understand, they're desperate. They really don't want this to happen, they'll do anything to stop it. You've got to come help me, Joe. You've got to come kill me. Now, before they get to you."

"Somebody wants to stop me from killing you? By killing me? This makes no sense."

"No, no," she shook her head impatiently. "Not just that. Keeping me alive is only the side effect." She looked over her shoulder again. "I've got no time. You have to hurry, Joe. You've got to take care of – Joe, they're coming. And they're going to keep on coming until they stop you. Until they stop me. I – " and the hologram cut out.

"Bah!" Joe spat into the empty night. Well, so much for his beauty sleep. He lay in bed for a couple of minutes thinking things over. "Damn it, lady." He got up and activated his apartment's enhanced security measures, swung by the fireplace and then went back to bed. He picked his Sunfire 35 up off the sheets, stared at it for a moment, then put it in the drawer of his night table.

He gave the night one last, long listen, heard nothing, and closed his eyes.

Chapter 7

The first alarm woke him up. The second one lifted him out of bed.

The first one, a low soft beep, was his early warning system. Somebody had come through the front door of the apartment building. Joe wasn't the only person who lived here, and the soft chime had woken him several times during the night.

The second alarm, a slightly louder chime accompanied by a flash of bright light from the strobe mounted in the corner of his ceiling, took him out of bed. That was the close perimeter alarm. Someone was standing outside his apartment door.

Joe had three minutes to get into position. The array of locks on his apartment door would stop the best lock man for three minutes. He was already dressed – he'd slept in his clothes – and moved silently from the bedroom into the living room, keeping the lights off. He checked the front door. Still closed. He listened hard in the dark for the telltale scratch and blip of someone trying the locks – no sound. Were they just standing there looking at his door?

"You may turn on the lights if you wish," said a voice from the dark.

Despite himself, Joe jumped. "Respectable security," the voice continued, low and sonorous. Even in the dark Joe could see the man sneer. "The locks took me ten seconds instead of my usual five."

All right then. Joe stood up from his instinctive crouch and slapped the wall panel to half light. The room illuminated enough to show the man sitting in Joe's favorite chair. Tallish, dressed in next year's suit, so incredibly wrinkle free and clean Joe figured it was electrostatically charged. The guy looked like an investment ad, polished and precise and completely trustworthy with whatever task you set him to.

Even though he was sitting, suit man wasn't relaxed. He was still. Preternaturally still, like the tiger who'd just found the rabbit.

"Okay, so you can handle locks," Joe said. He stood easy and gestured at the kitchen. "Beer?"

The guy showed his first wrinkles, on the bridge of his nose. "No thank you," he said with emphasis. "Quite frankly I have far, far better things to do. I have been given this task at very short notice, so let's get it over with." His eyes moved, flicking up and down Joe's length. "You have let yourself go, Captain Drive. But still, you appear to have rebuffed our request this morning to cease and desist whatever actions you have planned." He paused and lifted an eyebrow. "Do you have any actions planned? Any travel in your future?"

"Haven't the faintest idea what you're talking about," Joe said, and left it at that.

The man considered it and shrugged. "There's always the possibility, of course, that a man of your talents could have transportation available. A spacejet stashed away somewhere for a rainy day. We simply cannot take that chance."

"We?" Joe asked.

The man scowled minutely, as if a fly had landed on his dinner. "I do not act alone, Captain Drive. But, as I said, I have bigger and better things to attend to. So, let us conclude this little endeavor. I require your assurance, Captain Drive. Your absolute assurance that you have taken your – visitation – for the nonsense that it is, and have no thought whatsoever about taking any action or travel based on what you have heard or what you may have thought."

"You mean, do whatever crazy, insane thing that the crazy lady asked me to?"

The man nodded, relaxing just the tiniest bit.

"Well that," Joe continued, "is entirely my business, now, isn't it?"

The man blinked and said, "This isn't going to be as straightforward as I assumed. I am authorized to encourage you." He turned his right hand palm-up and waved the fingers of his left hand over top of his wrist.

Joe saw the thin edges of a hologram flicker in the air above his hand. Another wallet implant. He heard his own wallet give a soft ping from the bedroom.

"I understand you live on a military pension," suit guy said. He swept a hand around the apartment. "Obviously not the finest of incomes. This will help considerably. It will also help you to forget anything the woman told you and anything you may consider doing about it. Correct?"

Joe pretended to mull it over. If nothing else, this crazy venture was padding his bank account. But money wasn't everything, or so his mother had tried to tell him. Besides, he'd already seen his account emptied just as easily. Underneath and behind the small amount of greed warming his belly was another emotion that had now gone well beyond irritation.

"I see. Or, no doubt, dire consequences will ensue." The man shrugged again, a single lifted shoulder. "That's all you need? My promise?" Joe continued. "And for that you dragged your sorry Elite ass away from whatever you've got planned to slum it down here to my place, walk through my security, sit in my chair and be as threateningly non-threatening as you know how to be?"

The man nodded. "And your answer is?"

"Complicated," Joe replied. "First off, I don't like being threatened. I don't know a single soldier who does. You should have known better. Second, I don't like you. You're arrogant. You assume too much. At the very least, you could have knocked and waited to be let in."

No sign from the guy opposite. No emotion at all.

"Third, you're Elite to the very core."

"You're part of the Interstellar Space Force," the man replied. "Every soldier is considered an Elite as well. Especially the officers."

Joe felt his face get red and was powerless to stop it. "That's a pretend designation and you know it as well as I do," he snapped. "Every Lowlife soldier wants to consider himself an Elite. That's part of the recruiting spiel. You guys toss us a few crumbs, smile at us a few times to perpetuate the illusion, but you and I know different. Most officers know different. Soldiers aren't Elites. They're Lowlifes with pretentions. Did you walk in here and greet me like an old friend? A colleague? No. You waltzed into my apartment and sat down in my chair. Every fiber of your being says that you really want to scrape me off the bottom of your shoe. And if all that wasn't enough, you forgot the most important thing of all."

This time the man raised both eyebrows. "Yes, Captain

Drive? Do tell."

Joe jabbed a finger in the air towards him. "I. Want. To be. Left. Alone."

The man nodded and rose from the chair. He reached out to shake the wrinkles out of his wrinkle-free jacket. "I see. Very well, then. I will take your promise as assumed and be leaving."

He took a step towards the door, pivoted, and before Joe could see the draw a laser gun was in his hand. It was dark, sleek, a Nova, tipped with a red beryllium crystal. Powerful enough to go through Joe, his apartment wall, and the three apartments behind him.

Joe had no time to move and didn't bother trying. The man squeezed the trigger. Looked down at his weapon and squeezed it again.

Joe smiled. "Dampening field," he said. "You can't even buy one on the black market. But an ISF quartermaster owed me a favor." He reached for the small of his back.

The man was fast, leopard fast. Joe's reflexes launched him into a scrambling retreat, but the heel of the guy's hand grazed his chin, a stinging blow that watered his eyes. His momentum propelled him backwards, but the man – the assassin, Joe realized – already had a foot behind his leg. Joe went down hard, right hand trapped beneath him.

He saw a flicker in the room's semidarkness. A blade. The killer came down out of the sky, all six and a half feet of him, point of the knife headed for Joe's eye. Joe wrenched himself to the left. The knife scraped the back of his skull as his right hand came free.

A short, sharp bark tore through the apartment. A blast of flame arced out from his hand. The man lifted off him, sailed back and crashed to the floor. Joe snapped to his feet again, feeling the burn at the back of his head, shaking off the ache in his right wrist from the recoil of the Smith and Wesson Model 19 revolver.

He waggled the ancient relic in the air as he stood over the dying assassin. "Dampening fields shut down lasers," he explained, "they don't stop lead."

The hole in the guy's chest was precise, a little off center, oozing blood through a rip in the fabric that was blackened around the edges. Although he couldn't see it, Joe knew that the hole in the guy's back was an entirely different story. .357 Magnums tended to make a mess. Bits of the assassin were dripping off Joe's ceiling and wall.

"Comfortable in the hand," he continued as he placed the antique back on the mantelpiece, "but damn, I hate the cleanup."

The guy was beyond talking, so Joe didn't bother asking anything. Just waited another three breaths until the assassin took his last. He said "Damn," to the night and turned the lights on full. Then he grunted onto his hands and knees to pat the guy down.

"Okay, let's see who you are," he muttered. No ID. Just the two weapons, knife and Nova, both of which Joe tossed into the corner for later filing downstairs. Transpo card and no wallet. Joe felt around the corner of his arm and found the holographic wallet implant just under the guy's wrist, a flattish disc about an inch across. Impressive. He'd heard of the tech, but hadn't run across it before Ella's appearance yesterday.

After going through the pockets he gave the corpse a more thorough pat down - hair, collar, armpits, ribs, waistband - and, after a moment's consideration, crotch. Tucked up along the guy's inner thigh Joe felt a long, hard, oblong something.

"Another implant?" Joe said to the night. "You have got to be kidding me." Still, it had to be checked out. He retrieved the guy's knife and slit open the trousers. The aggressively smooth fabric parted with a sigh to reveal, not a stainless steel cock, but a black wedge taped to the guy's skin.

Joe peeled it off. It had some heft, more than you'd expect from its size. The wedge was long enough to fit across his palm, thumb-thick at the large end, tapered down to a smooth line at the other. Rounded edges, burnished to a dull sheen. It looked to be made of black ceramic, or maybe some kind of rock. Iron? It had the weight of it, and more. He looked it over carefully. No writing, no markings of any kind. He'd never seen its like. He slipped it into a pocket.

"Damn," he said to the night again. Stony and Everest had taken care of the morning body. This one was all up to him.

Suit guy had expired on top of the only nice carpet in the apartment, a Persian number that Joe had picked up on an Earthside shore leave to Tabriz. Now he eased it out from under the furnishings. With a curse of regret he rolled the guy over to one edge, then kept on rolling until the carpet made a fat sausage that Joe could just barely manage to lift.

He heaved it up, squeezed out the door and hoofed it to the nearest transport link. He used the transpo card that he'd found in the guy's pocket and fuzzed them both over to the bluff overlooking the mine. He walked to the edge, unrolled the carpet and watched as the corpse tumbled down a half mile of sharp lunar rocks, shredding itself to bits along the way. He'd get rid of the carpet somewhere else on his trip home.

Dawn was breaking over the crater rim by the time he got back to his apartment. Joe finished cleaning up the mess on the walls. When he was done he said, "Damn," once more into the quiet of his formerly peaceful life. Then waved his console awake and booked a ticket for Mars.

Chapter 8

He wasn't doing the job. Far from it. But this mess had brought a capable killer to his living room and he still didn't know what the hell was going on. In the absence of straight answers from Ella, he needed on-the-ground intel. He used up some more of Ella's expense account and booked himself a first-class berth on the 7 p.m. spacejet to Canal City.

No better place to find out more about the Pounds. Look straight up from anywhere in the glittering Martian jewel of a city and you'd be staring at Poundville. Besides, Joe knew a guy.

Once their two sons and daughter began to arrive, Wheeler Pound's wife had pestered him for a bigger place to live. In typical Pound fashion, he'd gone big. He threw a magnetic lasso around a nice-looking asteroid and tugged it into orbit around Mars. The day after he stationed it in synchronous orbit above Canal City, forever changing the night view and causing a month of dust storms all over the red planet, the shocked Home Alliance government back on Earth brought in rules to prevent it ever happening again. But Poundville was already in place, and there it stayed.

Wheeler brought in the Peter Foundation to boost the

rock's gravity to Earth-normal with one of their fancy devices, then set about terraforming his paradise. In short order Poundville was draped in a lush atmosphere and covered by rolling countryside dotted with large mansions, small towns and a lake. Wheeler ran his business interests from Poundville. As far as anybody knew he hadn't been off the rock for the past ten years.

Joe had never been to the Pound family enclave, but he'd seen plenty of Canal City during his time with the Interstellar Space Force. Starjumper Base was only a short hop over the horizon. Canal City was the first port of call for soldiers on leave.

Of course, he'd seen plenty of the rest of Mars, too. The planet was pockmarked with mines, quarries, factories and smelters. Lowlife towns squatted like mushrooms around the edges of the industrial zones, providing the workers that kept industry going.

Those towns also served as hubs of operations for the Resistance. Isolated groups of disaffected workers, seeking to disrupt the Martian economy and send a message to the Home Alliance on Earth, had tried to harm the mines and factories for years. Joe had seen those towns from the seat of his spacejet bomber as he'd dropped precision munitions from the stratosphere onto rebel positions far below. His bombs had been targeted to individual buildings, sometimes single people.

Before they'd been reprogrammed mid-flight to be something else entirely.

He booked a room at one of Canal City's hotel casinos for three days. That would be long enough to find out whatever he could about this mess. And he knew just the person who could help.

Miles Crookshanks was a velvety-smooth con man with

great fashion taste and an excellent nose for information. He had tried to interest a much younger Joe in a vacation property on the back side of Phobos one evening over a few hands at the blackjack tables. Joe, who had flown over the back side of Phobos, didn't take it personally, and the two became friends. As Joe moved up the Space Force ranks and did occasional investigative work, Miles had proven to be a good source of the type of information that didn't make the holo reels. In particular, Miles had found it both profitable and wise over the years to keep tabs on the Solar System's most influential family.

Joe didn't own any luggage except for his old ISF duffel. He'd never traveled anywhere after arriving on the Moon. He picked up an overnight bag and a few essentials at an import store close to his apartment, then went back to pack some underwear, a selection of his nicer clothes, and – after careful consideration – nothing from his downstairs bunker. This wasn't the kind of mission that required heavy weapons, and he'd never get them past spaceport security.

If he did need specialized equipment, he knew who in Canal City to get it from. But then, she'd be as likely to burn him with a laser as hand it to him. He'd keep a low profile. Get in, get the intel, get out. No reason to bump into Kate at all.

The black wedge created an oversized dent on his bedspread where it lay next to his overnight bag. Curious little thing. Joe had some time before his flight, and Miles Crookshanks wasn't his only source of information. He pocketed the wedge and spent an hour walking over to North Heaviside, where the street sweepers kept the Moon dust at bay and back-alley dealings had gone way underground.

North Heaviside was farthest away from the mine, and worked hard to get farther away still. The houses here were custom built, no prefabs, with architectural highlights that ran the gamut from Kyoto pagoda to Tuscany villa, in every color imaginable except for Lunar Grey. They were owned by the city's shop owners, business executives and politicians, everyone in the city who had pretensions to live like Elites. They woke late and socialized late, held fancy dress balls and posed for the holo lenses. But Joe had watched them, like everyone else in Heaviside, and like everyone else he saw through the thin lie. The residents of North Heaviside still frowned at their account balance when they paid the bill. The holos of their parties were seldom aired beyond Heaviside itself. Rebel graffiti never stayed for long on the sides of the expensive shops, but the growing rumble of the Resistance made North Heaviside nervous and jittery.

Joe disapproved of the false arrogance, but came over to North Heaviside when he needed to buy something nice.

He turned down a quiet avenue off Cassiopeia Boulevard. He walked through the third shop door into a small, tastefully-appointed keyhole of a store called Little Things. Tiny shelves dotted the walls like scattered leaves, barely large enough to hold a holo projector for the sales pitch and the miniscule products themselves. Etched words over the front section said Remote Surveillance, where the shelves held watchers and listeners almost too small to see. Further down the wall was Healthcare, featuring nanobot self-diagnostic kits and microhormone pumps to fine-tune your love life. Lifestyle Enhancement came next, then Lightly Used, where the cases on the shelves looked a bit ragged.

Simon fiddled with something under an oversized magnifier behind the desk at the far end. Simon had cleaned up pretty nice, Joe thought. The boy's blond hair was stylishly messy but clean, the semi-silk shirt color-matched to the store and to a pair of shoes that Joe was pretty certain you couldn't get Moonside. Little Things looked good on him.

A far cry from the empty quarry where Joe had convinced a loan shark not to send Simon through the rock crusher.

Simon looked up from his work, his salesman's bright smile fading to something sadder and more real when he saw who had come in. "Mr. Drive man," he said, standing to bump knuckles, "too long, too long. Glad to see you out of The Shaft."

"You're looking good, Slide," Joe said, using Simon's street nick. "You've gone upscale. New threads, better merch. The place looks great. So do you."

Simon went back to his showroom grin, the brilliant display of charm that lit you up from the inside and made you trust the guy. That charisma had landed him in the rock quarry. Now it had got him here. He waved his arm about the place. "All thanks to you, Drive, and don't you know it. Need anything? Just ask."

Joe threw his arms out wide to match Simon's gesture, then pulled the kid in for a surprised hug. "For starters," he whispered into Simon's ear, "how about turning off the store security? Maybe erasing the last two minutes?"

Simon stepped back from the embrace, said, "Wait here a second, please, there's something I have to attend to." He disappeared through a hidden door and was back a moment later. "All right, Drive man, we're alone." He pointed a pen at the storefront and the windows opaqued. Joe heard the door's maglock hum to life. "And we won't be disturbed." He grinned again. "So, Joe Drive has left The Shaft and now he wants a private moment. Special day, man. I'm all chills."

Joe laughed. "No biggie, Slide, there's nothing going on. I'm here to ask a favor, that's all."

"Shoot."

Joe pulled out the burnished black wedge and held it up. Then watched with amazement as, over the next three seconds, Simon did the most amazing dance. The first second was casual curiosity as he leaned in for a closer look. The next second was given over to sheer, wide-eyed terror as he executed a full-body recoil from the wedge. By the third second, in an impressive display of control, Simon mastered his reflexes, stopped his flight and settled for wary alertness.

"Tell me the story," he said.

Joe gave him the short version. "I got involved in something. It brought a bad man to my door last night. He had this thing in his pocket. Now your turn," he finished. "Something about this trinket gave you the screaming jeebies just now. What is it?"

Simon hadn't taken his eyes off the thing, but hadn't gone near it, either. "So a bad man shows at your place and the next thing you're going through his pockets? Pretty sure you left out some detail, my man, but hey, whatever. As for this – I don't know," he muttered, distracted. "It looks like something I'd had described to me once, that's all. But it couldn't be. Mind if I capture it?" He brought out a miniature holo camera from behind the desk.

Joe nodded and Simon set up the camera for a 360 scan. "I'm going to ask a friend, and I'll get back to you soon. Two things, Mr. Drive."

"Launch them," Joe said.

"Put it back in your pocket and keep it there, safe and hidden. Don't pull it out or wave it around, not for anybody. And second thing. Don't ever call it a trinket again. I have a feeling it's a whole lot more than that."

Joe knew a hedged bet when he heard one. "Come on, Simon, what is it? You know something."

"No I don't know anything, and what I suspect just isn't possible. Let me do some digging. I owe you that. I'll be in touch soon." Simon inched towards him as he spoke, not even aware he was doing it. Joe recognized the signal. Simon was pushing him towards the door.

"Okay, all right," he turned to go. "This really is a nice store you have, Slide. I'm glad things are working out for you."

"Thanks," Simon said as he pressed the button to unlock the door. "But it's Simon now. I'll call you. Bye." Joe was on the street. He heard the maglock clunk once more behind him. Little Things was closed for the day.

Feeling distinctly more aware of the wedge's weight in his pocket, Joe headed for home to grab his bag.

Chapter 9

Joe walked back across town to The Shaft, retrieved his overnight bag, and hovered for a moment before closing the door. He gazed at the homey living room, with its slate fireplace and mountain cabin décor. He hadn't been anywhere for three years. A small knot of nerves rolled around in his gut.

"Stupid," he muttered, and locked the place tight. It was an information-gathering recon mission to satisfy his curiosity. Nothing more than that.

The air had become unusually clear and crisp. The climate planners must have kicked the dust scrubbers into high gear. He stood outside his apartment and found himself taking a deep breath on the sidewalk. They'd boosted the oxygen level under the dome, too, an unexpected and rare treat. Joe decided to walk, slinging his travel bag onto one shoulder. He headed out of The Shaft to where the houses grew thin on the ground, then out onto the rough, silver flats east of the city.

His last commercial space flight had been three years before. The memories of that day leaped into his mind as he saw the first streaks of light from departing spacejets at Heaviside Port. He'd stormed into the officer's galley at Starjumper Base, fresh off the mission that had opened his eyes, and smashed a fist into Commander Blinken Garfield's face. He remembered feeling the man's nose break. He'd ripped the crossed thrusters off his captain's uniform, thrown them at Garfield and walked off the base. Hopped on the first commercial jet to leave Canal City and ended up on the Moon.

Others had chosen to walk this evening, too. He engaged a few of them in light conversation as they walked along. Safe topics, like the weather and the Crater Hoppers' chance in the upcoming Zero-Gball championships. He was careful to stay clear of topics like, 'Oh, how did you spend your night?' 'I killed and disposed of an Elite assassin. How about you?'

The spaceport was in the middle of its evening rush. Every few minutes a spacejet landed and another took off into the gathering dusk, rumbling the ground underneath. As the sleek, silver darts jumped away from the runways, climbed into the sky and then continued their arc to a ballistic vertical as they reached for escape velocity, Joe felt a ripple of excitement replace the nervousness behind his navel.

You're done with that, he reminded himself. Yeah, you were the fastest pilot in the known universe. So what. Fat lot of good that did everyone else.

The sidewalk got busier as he approached the spaceport. He passed by a cluster of transpo booths humming and buzzing away as more people fuzzed in and joined the walkers. The sidewalk traffic grew uncomfortable. People were close now, occasionally jostling him. He was almost to the front door and reaching for his ticket when someone jostled him again.

No, not a jostle. A polite, light hand on his right elbow. "A word, Mr. Drive, if you don't mind," came a soft voice in his ear.

He turned and found himself looking at a monk. Or maybe a zero-Gball player with an affectation for grey robes. The young man hanging onto his elbow was a bit shorter than Joe, powerfully built, with a close-cropped head that made him look more like a fighter than a philosopher. He had the smooth face and glowing complexion of youth. Despite his broad shoulders the hand on Joe's arm was light and nonthreatening.

"I won't keep you from your flight," the stranger continued, "but I'd love a word in private. Please." He gestured, the robe flowing away from his other hand, at an alcove with a curved bench scooped into the side of the building.

Joe checked his instincts. The fellow didn't trip any alarm bells, so Joe went with him. The young man lowered himself onto the alcove bench, gesturing for Joe to sit opposite. Their knees practically touched. The bustle of the busy sidewalk faded to a quiet murmur.

"Thanks so much for agreeing to talk," said the stranger, his voice carrying effortlessly to Joe's ear in the tiny space. "It's important."

"And you are?" Joe inquired.

"My name is Ryza." His voice was light and soft, but there was a spark in the boy's blue eyes. Joe pegged him for maybe late twenties. "I'm from the Foundation. Perhaps you've heard of it."

"The Peter Foundation?" Joe snorted to cover his surprise. "Everybody's heard of it. Nobody knows anything about it. You're the gravity guys, right?"

Ryza laughed, loud in the tiny space but not noticed by passersby. "That's what we are famous for, I suppose. And to be fair, we don't advertise the rest of it." He leaned forward and the spark in his eyes grew brighter. "We are a future-forward organization dedicated to the betterment of humanity. We have a broad base of physicists, mathematicians, data scientists, xenobiologists, engineers, artists, and philosophers. Together we," he searched for the right word, "we keep an eye on things. We watch, Mr. Drive. Insert ourselves where we feel it is necessary. Invent certain things when they become useful. And yes, to use your turn of phrase, we are the gravity guys. We place Earth-normal gravity on any planetary or sub planetary body that requires it."

Joe nodded. "Well, right there, that's a lot more than I've ever heard about the Peter Foundation. So why are we having this little chat?"

Ryza laughed again, as if Joe had just proven him right on a bet. "Direct. To the point. As I suspected you would be." He slid his hands into his sleeves, a very monklike move. "We have arrived at a pivotal moment in the life of the Solar System, Mr. Drive. Understand, we at the Peter Foundation watch probabilities. We see what's going on and extrapolate likely outcomes from the equations. That's a simplistic explanation, but it will do for now. Suffice it to say that something big is afoot. And the Algorithm is clear that you will play a role in how things work out."

Joe scowled. He already had a crazy lady and some nameless assassins to deal with. The last thing he needed was a weird scientist with delusions of grandeur. "Look, kid, I don't care what your equations and statistics told you about me, but I have a plane to catch. So," he rose to leave.

"Oh, your plane won't be leaving without you. We gave it a faulty magrail, nothing major but enough to keep it grounded. It will be fixed the moment we're done here." Ryza looked concerned. "I've messed this up. And by the way, Mr. Drive, I don't interpret the Algorithm. The Council does, by way of the Foundation's Prognosticator. I'm a mechanical engineer by trade. But I am serious about something major happening, and about you being involved. The Algorithm is definite about that."

Hocus pocus and prophecies of doom. It was like he'd fallen prey to a tarot reader. Still, he had to ask. "And if I stay home and do nothing? Forget all this and lock the door?"

Ryza's face fell into a deep solemnity. "The Algorithm is clear on that one, too. 94% likelihood of a very bad outcome. Almost a certainty."

"What, like I'll have a bad day?"

"No, Mr. Drive. If the Algorithm is accurate, we all will."

A moment's silence passed through the alcove. "Okay," Joe said at last. "So why are you here, Ryza? I'm already headed for the plane. Why grab me and have this scary little talk?"

Ryza glanced down and the top of his shaven head turned pink. Was the kid embarrassed? "We are trained to watch, Mr. Drive. To be impartial observers and only intervene when necessary. Full disclosure, I wasn't told to talk with you. But, like you," and here he looked into Joe's eyes again, "I hate not knowing. Who are you going to see on Mars, Mr. Drive? Are you taking anything with you? Do you have a mission there? You see, our equations point to the importance of this moment, but we don't really know much detail." He slid his hands back into his sleeves. "My superiors call me inquisitive."

Joe nodded. "Yeah, the brass don't like it when you ask questions. I get that."

Ryza waited. Joe waited, too. The boy got the hint in pretty short time. Ryza rose to his feet. "I see my curiosity will remain unsatisfied. Enjoy your flight, Mr. Drive. Please. Good luck on Mars. Although I think your success will rely a lot more on skill than luck."

"And you'll be watching, I suppose?" The kid grinned, gave a long-sleeved wave and melted into the crowd.

Joe sat in the alcove another minute thinking about what he had just heard. Statistics. Math. A definite interest from the Peter Foundation in whatever the hell he was up to, an outfit that rarely had contact with anybody outside themselves. But nothing actionable. And nothing that was about to change his mind. Very well. He got up, hefted his bag and continued into the spaceport.

Chapter 10

Joe was shipping out on the Starlight Express. Ella's expense allowance had been more than generous, so he'd treated himself to a first class berth. The Starlight Express billed itself as the fastest passenger ride in the Solar System, Heaviside to Canal City in 8 hours 45 minutes, thanks to Earth and Mars being almost at conjunction in their orbits.

Joe had made the trip faster back in his Space Force days. But he was no longer behind the stick of an exotic, screaming rocket sled moving at 3 percent of the speed of light. He'd just have to make do.

"Welcome aboard, Mr. Fong," said the flight attendant, taking his overnight bag and storing it away for him. Joe had broken out the Fong ID for this trip and ducked into a washroom stall with a concealer kit before entering the spaceport. Now his hair was luxuriously long and white, his eyes sported epicanthic folds, and his skin tone was several shades darker. He nodded politely to the flight attendant and took his seat. It adjusted to his weight and contours, unobtrusively wrapping around his thighs and midriff to hold him in place.

Joe listened carefully to the preflight briefing. He doubted very much that he'd hear anything new, but he was curious to see how the masses were prepped for a spaceflight.

"In a few moments we will lift from the gantry," the flight attendant said. "You'll feel a sensation like a big hand is pushing you into the back of your chair. Don't worry, that's normal. It might be hard to breathe for a moment, and that's normal, too. Lift off will take 27 seconds, so just close your eyes and count. During most of our flight, passengers in the main cabin will have the delight of experiencing zero G's, or absence of gravity. Make sure your seatbelts are fastened! Enjoy our selection of Spaceman food." A ripple of laughter came from somewhere behind him.

Joe almost laughed himself. He'd had Spaceman food, and couldn't recommend it. But not tonight. Passengers in First Class were treated to Earth-normal gravity and excellent catering throughout the flight.

Which brought a question to his mind. He flagged down the flight attendant. "Yes, Mr. Fong?" she asked.

He added some scholarly breathiness to his voice."I am curious, how do you manage to keep gravity for one cabin and not another?"

The attendant smiled. "We have a Peter Foundation Device, of course. Way smaller than the planetary versions, but it can be marvelously tuned. Foundation engineers calibrate the settings for us every few months, we're not allowed to go anywhere near it. If we wanted to we could have the Foundation set it to ignore the row of seats behind you. Or even yours."

Joe whistled. "Precise. No thank you, I like my gravity."

The liftoff was as smooth as the parasilk on Ella's pyjamas. The seat formed and responded to his every move.

As the Starlight Express broke out of the Lunar atmosphere and spun on its axis to get ready for the jump, Joe watched the stars rotate outside his porthole window. He remembered their names and positions, completely unchanged in the three years since he'd last navigated by them.

Which was a hell of a lot more than he could say for himself.

The first glass of champagne – real, as far as he could tell – relaxed him into the flight. When his seat began unobtrusively giving him a massage he fell asleep. He woke when the seat snugged up around him in preparation for the rocket's pivot and burn down into Mars' gravity well.

The full night's sleep had been great, but he felt his insides sink along with the ship. He'd never planned on returning to Mars. It had only been three years; not nearly long enough for him to forget what he had done here.

The rocket settled down onto its gantry by the outskirts of Canal City. It was already midafternoon local time, which worked in Joe's favor considering the long night ahead. The place had grown since he'd left. He caught glimpses of it outside the spaceport windows as he did the arrival dance with the rest of the passengers.

Canal City, a sprawling metropolis of 15 million souls, was many things to many people. Financial hub for the outer planets; supply depot for prospectors heading to the asteroid belt; a center of learning, with half a dozen excellent universities and libraries; and, doing more for the local economy than all the rest, the gambling hub of the Solar System. Almost 50 huge casinos ringed the city core, most of them paired with towering hotels.

Joe set himself up in the Red Zone, a middling grade hotel casino complex. Not the best, by far not the worst. He checked in under Mr. Fong's alias and disguise. With any luck the facial recognition cameras would gloss over him like they did a thousand other visitors every single day.

After a decent hotel meal and another solid nap, he cashed in more of his expense account and hit the casino floor. This would be a true test of the Fong disguise. Every inch of the floor was covered by surveillance. If anyone with so much as a blemish on their record showed their face in a Canal City casino, security knew about it. The word would go out, and people like Joe would feel a ripple go through the room.

He won some money at baccarat, lost a little at blackjack, made a little bit more at the roulette wheel. Gambling had never been Joe's thing but he had a mind for math. Although he was careful not to count cards or do any of the other silly tricks that would get him kicked out of the place, he had a basic understanding of the odds that gave him just enough of an edge. As the evening wore on and he allowed himself a few drinks, Joe actually found himself enjoying the crowded space. He was having fun.

Around midnight he felt the invisible ripple and knew that Miles Crookshanks had entered the room. His old friend's reputation as a smooth operator had always preceded him. Nothing really changed on the casino floor. Most of the casino's patrons wouldn't have seen the blackjack dealer's head cock minutely to one side as the speaker in his ear whispered something. A drunk in a rumpled suit, sitting at the bar not far away, sat up and looked a lot less drunk. One of the servers surfing the crowd with a drink-filled tray brushed her waistband with her free hand, no doubt the hiding place of some nonlethal but very effective weapon.

Joe gave Miles another five minutes to settle into the baccarat table. Then he nodded to the blackjack dealer, got up and cycled over to the seat next to his friend.

The croupier welcomed Joe with a gracious wave and

slid cards from the boot across the green felt. Joe ignored Miles and played three chips on the table. He lost the hand and replaced his wager with three more. He won, collected his winnings and replaced the chips with another two. After he lost again he folded his interest in the game, said farewell to the croupier and left.

He cashed in his chips, went back to his room – room 332 – and waited. Thirty minutes later came a polite knock at the door. The view plate showed Miles, leaning on his signature ivory-tipped cane, accompanied by a redheaded stunner in a sequined dress. The two of them came in when Joe opened the door. Miles limped a bit more than he used to, Joe noticed, and used his cane more. They shared a rib-crushing hug and warm welcomes as the redhead waited.

Miles looked much as Joe remembered him from the old days: trim, tall, with sandy brown hair and grey just touching his sideburns. Holo star good looks, only accentuated by the years.

"Mr. Fong," he said at last, "allow me to introduce Emily. Emily, this is Mr. Fong." Joe, who had kept his disguise on, gave Emily a small bow.

In a gravelly baritone Emily said, "Pleased, I'm sure," and stepped over to the bar to help himself.

Joe grinned at the excellent performance. "Never could stay away from the boys, Miles. Or from trouble, I gather. I felt your arrival tonight. Seems like the casinos still keep a close watch on you."

Miles sighed and lowered himself onto the sofa. "The sins of my youth, it seems, are but slowly forgiven. At least they still let me enter."

"They keep a closer watch than you might think," said Emily, sipping a bourbon sour. "Hotel security tops up my pay to occasionally report back to them." Miles deftly slipped a chip into Emily's hand, who dropped it into a tiny sequined handbag. "So, what did we talk about tonight?"

Joe grinned, impressed, and came up with suggestions. "What do you say, Miles, reminiscing about old times? New business deal? Long lost brothers?"

Miles considered, leaned an elbow back on the sofa and said, "Let's do the business deal. Mining, of course, that's still the biggest game in town. You're a prospector with a line on a new asteroid, long-range spectrograph says it's full of americium and europium. Want to see if I can help make the connections." He glanced over at Emily.

"Sounds good," Emily said. He tipped his glass in their direction, headed for the bedroom and closed the door.

"Hope he's not doing anything personal in there," Joe commented.

Miles grinned again. "That's for my bedroom, not yours."

Joe laughed. "How's that leg of yours doing?"

"As good as it will ever be, I guess you could say," Miles answered with a slap on his bad knee. "A permanent reminder to always choose the winning side."

"Hey!" Joe said, "how was I supposed to know the informant had a friend? I'm just glad we got out of there alive."

They clinked glasses, toasted to lucky endeavors, and sat down. Miles twirled the head of his cane and gave Joe a look. "It's awhile since you've been this close to the action, old friend. I haven't seen you around here in almost three years. I heard you got the blinders removed from your eyes and it stung a little." His look withered a bit and he sounded hurt. "I heard it through the grapevine. Not from you."

"Sorry, guess I did leave in a bit of a rush." Joe frowned, sat up straight. "But I got the blinders pulled off? Is that what you think? Miles, they were getting me to– "

Miles held up a hand. "Turn of phrase, my friend, turn of

phrase. I know, believe me. It was a terrible job. But was it really that much of a secret? Oh, come on," he waved a hand as Joe rose up from his seat. "I don't mean to be harsh, but surely you must have known. There's no way you can drop bombs from above without collateral damage, no matter how precise they are."

The old anger was back, as bright and hot as a cerium flash bomb at max yield. "Collateral damage? Is that what you call it? There was nothing collateral about it, Miles. They tasked me to take out Resistance leaders and then lied to me about what the bombs did and where they landed. I thought I was taking out individual rebels. Precision removals, that's what they called it. They reprogrammed my loads in mid flight, Miles! Who could expect that?"

Miles lifted the hand off his cane in mock surrender. "Okay, okay, we're not here to discuss old times, I'm sure. We can't keep our Emily cooped up there for too long, although I have to say he really does prefer the bedroom. Your message said you need something. What is it?"

Joe had been ready to say more – much more – but Miles was right. Their time was short. He took a breath to calm down, flipped out his comm screen, opened up a notes app and scrawled across it with his fingertip. 'Pounds,' said the screen. 'Ella Pound,' he added.

Miles looked at it, considered, reached over and hit the delete button. 'Pretty big topic,' he wrote back. 'Narrow it down a little?'

Joe thought about it. Then he scribbled, 'Pound Asteroid security. Location of Ella.' After another moment he added, 'Any connection between Pounds and Peter Foundation.'

Miles' eyebrows went up. "My, my. Three years of nothing and then this? You do go fishing in deep waters, my friend. That explains a thing or two."

"Like what?" Joe asked.

"Small things. Didn't even register until now." He frowned into his drink. "A few extra eyes in the casino tonight. Your name came up in conversation yesterday, nothing consequential, just someone wondering whatever happened to you. A mention of something happening Moonside that had people nervous. Roll it all together, and I'd say there's some heat on you, my friend. As for this," he gestured to the screen, "I'll see what I can do." He reached over, hit delete again and then did his own scrawl. 9 p.m. tomorrow.

Joe hit delete and nodded. "It's good to see you, Miles," he said. "If I get a minute during this trip, let's catch up."

"Yes, definitely." Miles took a sip and flashed those innocent eyes over the rim of his glass. "Speaking of catching up, are you going to see her?"

Joe felt the weight of his past get a little closer. He gazed at the window overlooking Canal City, and beyond it to three years ago. "I don't know. Maybe."

Silence filled the space for a few minutes. Then they toasted to old times. Miles gripped the top of his cane and levered himself to his feet. "Okay Emily, time to go." The bedroom door opened. Emily emerged, smoothing a wrinkle out of his dress. No, Joe realized, not a wrinkle. Emily glanced back and winked as Miles closed the door behind them.

A sleep and a nap and he still felt drained. He wasn't used to this anymore. Joe finished his drink, found the bedroom undisturbed, and collapsed onto the soft hotel pillows.

***

In the deep reaches of the night he woke up and she was there. "Joe?" Ella said, her voice soft. "Sorry to wake you, I know it's late again."

"I'm getting used to it," he grumbled, and sat up. He blinked a few times to clear his vision. She was sitting on the edge of his bed again, and again in those mauve silk pyjamas. He bunched up the sheets around his midsection. "Nighttime for you, too, I see."

"Of course. Poundville is in geosynchronous orbit above Canal City. We're in the same time zone."

He woke up some more. "I didn't say I was traveling, how did you know – ?"

She shrugged. "I'm a Pound. Pound Enterprises, remember? If you travel, we know. And I'm so glad you're coming to help." She looked anything but glad. In fact, to his eyes she looked resigned to her fate.

"I'm not here to do anything, Ella. Except ask questions, since we keep getting interrupted. I need to know what's going on here." He got out of bed and reached for some clothes.

"I think we have some time now," she said. "Ask me anything."

"Okay." He squared to her. "Why the hell do you want to die?"

She sighed, the resignation in her face deepened by something else. Dignity? "I don't want to die, Joe, not even close. But I have to. It's the only way I can help the Resistance."

What? He hadn't seen that coming. "You lost me, lady. Back up a few steps."

Ella frowned. "Of course. Well, you know how the rebels have become stronger over the past year or so? They've gotten louder, attracted more recruits, even won more skirmishes against the ISF? And then, a couple of months ago, they seemed to be losing again?"

He shook his head. "Nope. I'm not much for the holo

reels these days." In fact, he'd totally forsaken any news of the outside world since the day he'd left the ISF and landed in Heaviside.

She looked startled. "Well, I suggest you turn on the reels and get reacquainted with your world, Mr. Drive. The Pound Endowment has always helped those in need, and in recent years that's mostly been victims of the war against the Resistance. I came to realize how deeply my family was involved in that war. Of course we benefit from a peaceful, orderly Solar System, but it's more than that. I saw that most of our businesses, especially mining, were run off the backs of the Lowlifes. The very people who are now pushing for their freedom." She leaned into the holo lens. "Do you see, Joe? My father benefits from the war against the rebels. In fact, I think he may be driving it."

Joe whistled into the night. "So you repurposed the Endowment, didn't you?"

She nodded. "Yes. I began directly supporting the Resistance with whatever they needed. Medicines. Transport. Spacejets. Even weapons. All very quietly. For awhile it made a difference. The rebels gained the upper hand. Then my father discovered what I was doing. He stopped all investment in the Endowment at once, of course. He's imprisoned me on Poundville, no contact with anyone. I'm under guard, watched by a lifebot to make sure I don't do anything stupid, and a contingent of soldiers so no one gets near me. I'm under house arrest. I need you to come – set me free."

"All right," said Joe, "that's the story. Now answer the question. Why die?"

"Isn't it obvious?" She shook her head, more to herself than him. "No, of course it's not. The Pound Endowment is out of funds, Joe. They can't help anyone anymore, not without my face on the holos and my presence at the fundraisers. The family money has ended. The only hope the Endowment has – that the Resistance has – is my will."

"Whoa. You mean, your inheritance goes to the Endowment?"

"Every credit of my personal wealth, which is considerable. It's ironclad, no way for my father to contest it. So you see, Joe, I really don't want to die. It's just the only way now that I can help." And, Heaven help him, she began to cry.

"Well. Um. Okay, thanks for that. Second question. Why me?"

Ella rallied herself and took a breath. "Yes, right. It's the security, Joe. This is Poundville. Everything – " her image faded and she looked alarmed, glancing down out of frame. "We're out of time. I'm out of time. Hurry, please."

And she was gone.

***

"Well, shit." Joe sat for a minute in the darkness of his bedroom, listening to the soft hush of hotel air conditioning in the middle of the night. He was awake now, electrified by Ella's revelations. He went over what she'd said and realized she had given him good advice. He knew very little about what had happened in the Solar System over the past three years. He'd kept himself out of touch, and now it put him at a distinct disadvantage.

"Intel is king," he heard Garfield's raspy voice drill into his ear on a long-ago training mission. "He with the better intel wins. The target, the surroundings, the situation. Learn everything you can, then find out what you don't know and learn that, too." Feeling more than a bit embarrassed, Joe went over to the hotel's console and flipped on the reels.

He spent an hour rolling through the major stories from

the last couple of years. News of the rebels and the ISF's fight against them headlined a majority of the reels. Ella was right. The rebels had made some gains – caved in a mine on Venus once they'd told the workers to leave, destroyed some infrastructure at a huge Mars factory complex, even won a full-on space battle against the Interstellar Space Force. The Resistance didn't seem to have a leader or figurehead – that would invite a bomb from someone like Captain Joe Drive – but to his trained eye they looked remarkably coordinated and disciplined. In scattered video shots of rebels in action the shadowy, indistinct figures moved with purpose and conviction, steadfast under fire.

The reels didn't portray them well, which was its own kind of news. According to the announcers the Resistance was made up of unkempt, disaffected rabble who took any opportunity to disrupt the careful harmony of the Solar System for no good reason. The Home Alliance, that happy and firm coalition of Earth governments that brought order and stability to both the home planet and the colonies, continued to guide the Interstellar Space Force in its efforts to quash the Resistance and keep everyone safe and happy. Under the Home Alliance's umbrella both Elite and Lowlife have experienced unprecedented prosperity, and they would not tolerate anyone who tried to ruin the party.

Right, Joe thought. As if the rebels were the ones bringing pain and suffering. He knew better.

One holoreel, shot from a drone, had zoomed in on an active battle. Joe watched it several times. A massive synthcrete plant in the Moon's southern hemisphere was under attack. The Resistance had brought up a sizeable force and were duking it out with an ISF guard base. Through the flurry of laser fire, rocket blasts and running figures, Joe saw some telling details. The rebels had impressive body armor, even full electroshields. Their front line assault was an intelligent, calculated diversion while a rocket cannon, somewhere in the dark craters behind them, lobbed charges deep into the facility itself, doing the intended damage.

When three rebels rushed up with a crate of new weapons, Joe froze the holo and zoomed in until the crate filled the bedroom. Emblazoned on the side was the Pound Enterprises crest.

Ella had done more than give the rebels funding. She'd stolen from her daddy's stockpiles to supply them with weapons. His estimation of her rose a notch.

Two months ago, just as she'd said, everything changed. The latest reels showed a string of ISF victories, complete with glowing play-by-play reports from the announcers. The Resistance was on its back foot, poised for a full retreat. According to the Home Alliance representatives, peace and order in the Solar System were just around the corner.

Joe stopped the holo in the middle of another battle – a rout, really, most of the fire coming from an ISF platoon towards a handful of rebels that ran into alleys and doorways to disappear. The angular, grey buildings were familiar. That was Heaviside, not very far from his apartment building. He thought back, glancing at the date of the recording. He remembered some extra noises in the night, a bit of buzz on the street the next day.

He'd rolled over and ignored it all.

Had his situational awareness deteriorated so badly? To have missed a full street battle within earshot of his home? The realization shocked him. He thought he'd been paying attention.

He dug a brew out of the room's pantry and sipped it till it was dry, staring out from the lightless room onto the streets of Canal City three floors below. What else had he missed? What else was he not seeing?

Chapter 11

The Martian day dawned soft and blue on the freshly-washed streets outside the hotel. Joe ordered room service breakfast and braced himself for what needed to come next.

Of course he was going to see her. Miles had known it before he'd asked the question, damn him. Like a moth had any choice about visiting a flame. He spent time with the bathroom mirror to make sure the Fong disguise was tight, then locked the room and headed outside.

He decided to walk to Kate's place. Canal City was beautiful and he needed the exercise. At least, those were the excuses he told himself. In truth – and he knew it damn well – he wanted time to figure out what he was going to say.

He bounced along the sidewalk, light on his feet, taking deep breaths of the Martian air. The Canal City engineers had used every rule in the playbook and invented a few more to make their city the playground of the Solar System. Somehow – Joe had no idea how all this worked – they had paid the Peter Foundation to rig the gravity in the place for slightly less than Earth normal. Not such a big difference that you failed to come down if you jumped, or found your wallet floating out of your pocket, but just enough so you thought the new workout routine must be doing some good. They'd also permanently boosted the oxygen in the entire city. He'd love to know how much that set them back.

The end result was gamblers who could go all night and feel good doing it, waking up the next day ready to do it all again. For Joe, it meant an easy stroll across town.

He walked into the middle of the Canal City financial district, awestruck all over again by its opulence. The Solar System's best architects had taken advantage of the light gravity to produce fantastic spires and totally improbable buildings that would have collapsed anywhere else. Most of the off-Earth finance came through these offices. Wealth was made here, counted here, moved here, sifted and sorted and picked through, siphoned into the pockets of those fast enough or smart enough to get it. Joe knew little of such things. But he did know that most of the people who ended up with the money were Elites. And most of the money was made off the backs of Lowlifes, who lived pretty much everywhere on the Mars colony except Canal City.

It was easy to forget amidst the glamour and the lie that he walked through, but Mars was still a colony. Like Venus, the Moon, and everywhere else that wasn't Earth, Mars paid tribute to the Home Alliance. Half of everything the planet produced went back to the tiny, distant green dot in the night sky on monthly shuttles. Half the income of everyone on the planet – save, perhaps, the Pounds – was taxed back to the Alliance. About the only thing that wasn't sent back to Earth was Lowlife children.

Those were needed for the factories and mines.

Few people occupied the sidewalks of the financial district this early in the morning. Joe mostly had the place to himself. It was a deceptive quiet, he knew. He spotted a patch of darker grey on the side of one building, half-hidden in the shadow of an alley. It was nothing now, but Joe knew what the paint covered. Underneath would be a field of stars in the shape of a crest, with a red fist breaking free from a blue-green one.

Even here, the Resistance had made its mark. The Lowlifes were getting tired of playing host to the Elites.

He passed by the building where Kate used to work. One of the more solid looking structures, it avoided the ephemeral architecture in favor of a look that told you the money managers inside were dependable and reliable. Kate had been a high level security analyst for the company, trained at all levels from close personal protection to urban anti-terrorism.

They'd met on a rescue mission. The CEO of a major bank had been kidnapped and spirited away to the tiny moon of Deimos, and he'd been the pilot on the ISF's hand-picked hostage retrieval team. When Joe and the rest of the team heard that a civilian was coming on board, a financial analyst no less, they'd rolled their eyes and braced for the worst. Kate strode through the door of the hangar in a form-fitting tactical jumpsuit that looked like it had received serious wear, outfitted with better gear than the rest of the team – comms, night vision, wall piercing vision, rappelling hardware, and even a fairly high wattage service laser strapped to her thigh. From the door of the hangar to the table where they were gathered she walked like she knew how to move in zero G boots and was perfectly at home in a situation briefing. By the time she got close enough to say, "Hey boys," the rest of the team had already assessed, glanced at each other, and given quiet nods.

The retrieval had not gone quietly. Joe dropped them outside the Deimos cave complex without incident, but the kidnappers had fortified their hideout with an impressive force shield. The second they touched it, incoming fire pinned them to the rocks. While Joe and his team did their best to keep the bad guys busy, Kate had whipped out some kind of a wire gizmo with antennas on it, stuck it into the force field, and studied the screen as a series of numbers and equations blazed by. Then she'd stabbed a single finger onto the keypad and stopped those numbers in their tracks. With a flurry of lightning code work she rewrote the force shield's protocols and opened them a door. Once she got them through it was all over but the shooting.

He and Kate, fresh off the high of the mission, went on their first date that very night. It hadn't ended for 18 months. Joe forgot to leave, and Kate forgot to ask him to. They each had their missions. Each of them occasionally got called away in the night. But they always laughed about it over drinks the next day.

Until that day, when he'd discovered the depth of Commander Garfield's betrayal. He'd arrived home after that fateful mission shaken, torn apart to his very core. He'd come through the door, broken Interstellar Space Force confidentiality and told her everything - the bombing run, what he thought he'd been doing, what he'd seen, everything.

She listened to him, accepted his silence when he ran out of steam, and thought about it. Then looked him in the eye and said, "Well, Joe, what did you think you were doing? That's the job. Pull yourself together."

It was like a slap in the face. Without another word, Joe had packed up his things and headed for the Moon.

Neither one of them had said a word to each other since.

Joe kept tabs on her every once in awhile, as he supposed she did with him. She'd moved up the corporate ladder, then built one of her own. She was now head of her own security and intelligence firm, competent as hell and well respected in the field.

She'd mostly kept her personal life out of the limelight. He'd seen one brief wedding announcement, with a small holo of a radiant Kate next to a decent-looking guy. He'd raised a toast and wished them well.

Joe remembered Kate's home address from memory. His feet bounced past the financial district into the realm of redstone townhouses and mansions, down quiet, tree-lined streets that cost the neighborhood a small fortune in water. The house looked much the same as he'd remembered, a detached single family affair that would have looked at home in Boston or New York City, right down to the white clapboard. The roof's shingles were slanted to shed winter snow that was never going to fall on Mars.

He flipped open his link, already keyed to her number. His thumb hesitated over the button. Was this a good idea? They'd had such a wonderful time until that one moment. She'd probably forgotten all about him. She had a new life now. She probably –

The door opened. "Well, are you going to stand there or come on in?" Kate asked from the front porch.

Joe went in.

Chapter 12

The interior of the place was like he remembered, but not. The smells were different. The same potpourri perfumed the mantelpiece over the moonrock fireplace, mixed with a tinge of the same cleaner the housekeeper always used. But now something masculine hung in the air. Pipe smoke? A hint of aftershave? Joe couldn't quite identify it, but it made him feel like an intruder.

The toys scattered over the corner of the living room identified the last smell for him. There was a baby in the house.

He heard her close the door, took a breath and started with small talk. "Always did like this neighborhood. How did you know I was out there?"

She snorted. "I run a security company, Joe. I received an alert when you were three blocks away."

Of course she would. "And the threat assessment?" he asked.

"Minimal. The AI had you pegged as a lost soul of a former boyfriend before you'd taken ten more steps."

Ouch. She beckoned him to one of the chairs. The

moment he sat down a black-suited figure glided into view from the kitchen. "Welcome back, sir," said the robobutler. "The usual?" Of course Jeeves would never forget.

"Thank you, Jeeves. That'd be nice."

"And for you, Ma'am?"

"I'll have what he's having," she said.

Kate waited him out. This was Joe's party, after all. He didn't let the silence stretch on for too long. "Listen, Kate, I know this is awkward, but – "

"It's been three years," she stopped him. "I have a different life now. My husband is out walking the baby, and what will be awkward is if you're still here when he gets back."

"Right." He felt his back stiffen up against the chair. Jeeves returned with two cut-crystal glasses, a finger of amber LaGrange Pure whisky in each, the drop of liquid nitrogen still creating tiny clouds over top. They both sipped. "I'm not here to mess with any of that. Really. The thing is, I need to ask for your help. Some things have happened, and I might be in a bit of a bind."

She took another drink, mulling it over. "So you're not here to – get reacquainted, or anything? You always did have a hard time letting go, and you've got a heart like soft cheese." Was that the ghost of a smile touching her lips?

"No, nothing like that. We had something, years ago. We've both moved on. I need intel, Kate. That's all."

She finished her drink and made a decision. "Intel. Advice. A good, swift kick. We'll see what you need. Okay, so give me the sit rep."

He laid it out for her – Ella's visit to Stony's, the assassin, his trip to Mars, Ella's explanation for her outlandish request. The only thing he left out was any mention of the black wedge. "It's totally nuts," he concluded, "so I came here to get some answers. I looked up Miles and asked him to snoop around. You remember him?"

"Your first dumb question. I'm a security expert in Canal City. Of course I know Miles."

"Oh. Right. The thing is," he shifted in his chair, aware how uncomfortable this would be to say, "I'm not sure I should trust him. We go way back, but – well, he's Miles. I'd just like a backup plan, that's all."

Kate snorted again. "I said I knew him. Miles Crookshanks would throw his mother onto a magrail if it gained him some advantage. Sure, I can help. Show me whatever he comes up with and I'll double check it for you."

"That's all I ask. Thanks." His drink done, he rose to go.

"Wait a second." Kate sighed. "Where are you staying? And where did you get that ridiculous disguise?"

Joe had forgotten he looked like an elderly Asian gentleman. He told her about the casino.

"The Red Zone? Not the worst choice, I suppose. But if Miles is dirty then he's in all the way, and they'll know who you are and where you live. And even if you didn't lose your cover through him, you probably blew it all to Hell by coming here."

Whoa. "Hadn't thought of that."

That shadow of a smile touched her lips again. "Yeah, well, I always could out-strategize you."

"Excuse me, ma'am." Jeeves was back, his smooth face canted into a picture of pained concern. "Security reports three hostiles approaching the house, currently four blocks out."

Kate considered this. "Threat assessment?"

Jeeves adopted a faraway look for a moment, then answered, "They are being unobtrusive about it, but definitely not friendly. Holding now at three blocks out. They are heavily armed." He pivoted to Joe. "I am afraid one of them has a holo of your disguise, sir." Back to Kate. "Shall I have them liquidated?"

That was a new word in Jeeves' vocabulary. Joe wasn't sure he wanted to know what that looked like. Kate said, "Not if they stay put at three blocks." To Joe she said, "Wait one."

She slipped into another room for a minute and came out with an access card and a thin, metal hoop with studs along the inner circumference. She clicked open the hoop, reached up and snapped it shut around Joe's neck. This time she smirked. "Always wanted to do that. The switch is under your left ear."

He reached up, found a small indent and flicked it. She nodded, then gestured to a mirror. "Have a look."

A slight haze had flowed up from the necklace to obscure his vision, but other than that the room looked normal. He moved over to the mirror. Standing on the other side of the glass was a youngish, scraggly, skinny 30-something with a gleaming temple implant and facial jewelry that Joe wouldn't have worn in a hundred years.

"Not bad," he said. "How long does it last?"

"Longer than you'll need it for. When you're done with it, just leave it in the apartment. This is a loan, not a gift." She handed over the access card and whispered an address in his ear.

He nodded. "Thanks, Kate. Thanks for everything." He swept an arm around to encompass the house. "I'm happy for you. Really." Although even he could tell that his heart wasn't in the words.

She gazed up at him. A heartbreaking mix of warmth and sadness breezed over her face. Then it vanished and she was the security company CEO again, serious and professional. "Nothing can touch you within two blocks of this house," she said. "After that you're on your own. Be careful, Joe. And whoever they are, don't let them find that apartment. It's a safe place and I want to keep it that way."

He nodded. Then, without giving Kate the hug he wanted to, Joe left, his boots clumping down the front walkway to the sidewalk.

Chapter 13

As Kate's door closed behind him, Joe stuffed his feelings into his back pocket and focused on the task at hand. He had a new disguise. He had an address to reach. And at least three soldiers to lose before he got there.

Kate's security was impressive. He couldn't spot a single surveillance precaution as he made his way out of the neighborhood. Jeeves had said that the men were holding at a three block perimeter. Maybe they knew about her protocols. Maybe not.

He turned at the end of the first block onto a busier avenue where the sidewalks, although not crowded, weren't empty. His best course of action was to walk right past them and trust to the disguise.

The first opponent was on his right. Just another dude loitering on the sidewalk, looking as non-threatening as a plainclothes soldier could get. He swept his eyes over the sentry as he walked past, giving the guy a wide berth and trying to give every impression of minding his own business. Half a block beyond the sentry he figured the disguise had done its work.

Another block closer to the downtown core and he wasn't so sure.

Two other men had materialized out of side streets and unobtrusively joined him on the sidewalk, about fifty yards back. By the time they all reached the next intersection he knew he'd been made. Two more of the team emerged out of shadows to cover him from the other side of the street. Keep going, Joe told himself, and tried his level best to pay them no heed and mind his own business.

He stole a glance in a shop window as he passed by. The necklace was still doing its job. The disguise was intact. What had given him away? He looked at the shop window again and realized his mistake. The disguise made him look like a scrawny, geeky man-child. His walk was erect, strong, and heel first, his boots making a loud clap on the pavement. The stride of a professional soldier.

He felt his training well up from the depths, Commander Blinken Garfield's voice loud in his ears. It had been the first day of a new exercise. He and a handful of pilots had stood with small packs in a bleak, arid corner of the backside of Mars. Joe remembered the thin air had been cold, and so had Garfield's black eyes."You are Space Force pilots. You will fly over enemy positions. Behind enemy lines. You will be sleek and fast and uncatchable. Until the day you're not. And when you get shot down, then you get to escape and evade."

For twenty days, through scrub forest and red desert and lush farmland and dark city alleys, they'd tried to avoid capture. Some aspects of that horrible training Joe had no use for here. He didn't need to live off the land, eat whatever came his way, find water, take shelter. He needed the urban version.

"When you're caught on the streets," Garfield had said, "find transportation. Spacejet. Hoverboard. Roller skates, if you have to. Steal a transpo card if you can. If you find a transpo booth you might be home free. Fuzz the hell out of there and keep on going."

No chance to steal anything, which left him with precisely one option. Joe fingered the evergreen transpo card in his pocket and broke into a cold sweat. He'd never actually seen how fast it updated itself. Never been keen to take the first trip into the mist, let alone a second one right away. He hoped the card's rejuvenation was practically instant. Regardless, he was about to find out.

The sweat trickled down the crease of his spine. A third of all molecular transport incidents – they called them incidents, not amputations or scrambled-egg executions – happened during transpo skipping.

A transpo booth had been slotted into the side of a building just up ahead. His tails were holding at least half a block away. Following, not trying to catch him. That was a question, but one that would have to wait for later. For now Joe would use the distance to his advantage.

He sidled over towards the edge of the sidewalk, closer to the transpo booth but not aiming directly for it. At the last moment, as he was about to walk past, he sidestepped inside, slammed his card up against the panel and hit the button. No programmed destination. He'd just use whatever coordinates the last person had left in the system.

The gray static opened up before him and he stepped through. The sound of shouts and running feet faded away behind him. He gave an involuntary shudder as his insides dissolved and he kept on going.

He was in a residential neighborhood somewhere on the outskirts of the city. He looked at his transpo card. Zero Credits, it said. "Come on, update." He gave it a shake. One Fare, Unlimited Distance. He turned around, stepped back into the transpo booth that had just spit him out, slapped his card against the screen and punched in random coordinates.

The gray static opened before him and he stepped through, just as the first of the tails came through the machine to try and find him. He had the weirdest sensation of passing through somebody else – a spine-chilling willie he wouldn't soon forget – and then he was at the spaceport. The move had gained him probably two seconds on his pursuers. The card updated again, he slapped it against the panel, punched in more coordinates and stepped through.

He was in a shopping mall, with a line of people waiting to use the booth. Without relinquishing the device and ignoring the howls of protest, he turned around, slapped his card against the panel and punched in more coordinates.

The Red Zone casino's main lobby. The numbers had fallen out of his fingers by reflex. Bad choice. More security was waiting for him there. A woman loitered by the street entrance. Another man looked through the holoreel he wasn't watching to scan the lobby traffic. They hadn't spotted him yet. He spun around in the booth, slapped his card against the reader and this time punched in coordinates that were completely random.

He fuzzed into a downtown bar. Drubbing music, crowds of people undulating to the beat. The place was space-themed, and hanging from the ceiling was an actual, honest to god SJ 37 Lightyear. The single seat, lightning-bolt deathtrap of a space jet had been his absolute joy to fly in the Interstellar Space Force. 'Wonder if that thing works,' he thought, then shook his head back to reality. One more slap against the panel, one more step through the fuzz and he came out at another section of the downtown core, into another booth embedded into the side of a tall, impossibly twisted building.

Joe stepped away from this booth and strolled over to a

side alley in between two buildings, tucked himself into the dark and waited.

Nothing happened. Five minutes. Nothing happened. Ten minutes. Still nothing. "I guess you taught me something useful, you asshole," he muttered into the dark.

He was about twelve blocks away from the address Kate had given him, an easy walk. He went to step out from the side alley and almost fell on his face as his left foot refused to move. A ventilation grate had caught the heel of his boot. His sudden departure had practically ripped it off the bottom of the shoe.

He took the shoe off, worked it free of the grate and inspected the damage. "That won't do," he said. He hopped over to the transpo booth, consulted a map and chose coordinates for a booth far on the outskirts of Canal City.

He emerged into another shopping district, but much different than the first. This one looked and smelled like Martian dust. Pressed sandblast walls provided a warren of corners and alcoves where innumerable stalls filled the open-air market. This was where Lowlifes came to shop, and business was brisk. People jostled past him as he exited the booth.

Joe felt himself relax. This was the Martian version of The Shaft. He spent a few minutes walking around, got some food from a stall that announced its presence with regular billows of steam, and eventually found the stall he was looking for.

An old woman, her skin as red as the Martian sand, sat behind a small anvil. An assortment of leathers hung on the wall behind her and the smell of glue filled the air. An ancient, miniature 3D printer huddled in a corner. She looked up from a book and stared at him.

"I have a job for you," he said, passing over the injured

boot. "And I'd like a bit of custom work done." He took out his wallet and fiddled with it.

A red light flicked on and off on a small console next to the anvil. The woman looked at it, checked the numbers on the screen, and cracked a smile. She took the boot, examined the broken heel. "For you, big man, I make anything you want."

By the time he got to Kate's apartment the small Martian sun was setting and Phobos had started another of its three daily swings across the sky. Directly above, Poundville gleamed in the distance like a small, green-tinged button against the velvet of the gathering night.

Chapter 14

The apartment was actually an elegant, blue-washed townhouse, tucked into a group of identical townhouses in a large, upscale neighbourhood on the side of a craggy hill. Joe admired the anonymity of the location and the great sightlines, then fished out Kate's key and let himself in.

The place was understated and gorgeous. The cushy furnishings, warm color scheme and top-drawer fixtures spoke equally of Kate's wealth and her obvious taste. He'd been so outclassed in their relationship. It was amazing they'd lasted as long as they did. Still, the kitchen was fully stocked and the bathroom had soft towels. He showered off the day, popped a beer and sat down on a couch that looked out over half of Canal City.

His link buzzed. He looked at it. The screen said the call originated from the most expensive brothel in Mare Dolce, a pleasure town on the nearside of the Moon. Joe had only been there once, and was sure nobody remembered him. He answered. The screen opened onto blank gray with a small box in the upper left hand corner. An arrow pointed to the box. Beside the arrow was written, Place Thumb Here.

That was new. Joe did as he was told. A moment later his phone confirmed his thumbprint. The blank gray screen shifted and swirled. Now the caller information said it was coming from the Vatican in Rome. This time there was a circle in the middle of the screen. An arrow pointed to it and the words next to the arrow said, Left Eye Here. "You've got to be kidding me," Joe muttered, but held the link up to his left eye and looked directly at the center of the circle.

The circle blinked, his identity doubly confirmed. The gray screen shifted again, this time showing an actual vista. Mountain tops, as far as the eye could see. According to his phone the caller was now on the top of Mount Everest. A familiar face slid into view.

"Hey, Simon," Joe said.

"No names. You alone?"

"Yeah."

"I mean, really alone."

"Yeah. What's with all the hocus pocus? I'm in a secure location."

"You're on flippin' Mars, man. How'd you get there?"

"Commercial spacejet, if you must know."

"Why?"

"That's my own business."

"Yeah. Well, whatever business you're in, it's about to get worse."

Joe cocked his head. "What the hell does that mean?"

"You got that thing you showed me?"

"Yeah."

"Show it to me again."

"Wait one." Joe came back after a minute and held it up to the screen. Simon peered at it. Shivered. Honest to god shivered, and said, "Flaming pulsejets, it's real. Now gently put it down. Let's chat."

Joe frowned, did as he was told and said, "Okay, so chat."

"What do you know about gravity?"

"If I hit you on the jaw you're going to fall down."

Simon made a face. "Not if I see you comin,' man. No, no, I mean like Moon gravity. Mars gravity, Venus gravity. You know what I'm talking about?"

"Oh," Joe said. "You mean the Peter Foundation."

"Yeah, what do you know?"

Joe sat back and thought for a moment. "Pretty much what anybody else does, I guess. The Peter Foundation was an obscure collection of scientist navel gazers out in the Peruvian desert. It was started by Peter somebody, forget his last name, with some nutty claim about guiding humanity through science. The Algorithm, he called it. Every once in awhile they'd come out with some nifty gadget, but other than that nobody paid them much attention.

"Then, about 80 years ago, a rogue space rock maybe a mile across sailed into the Solar System and brushed past Pluto. Pulled it right out of its orbit. That threw every government on Earth into a tizzy, because it was headed straight for us. In a month they formed the first version of the Home Alliance and tried to figure out how to destroy the thing.

"Then the Peter Foundation stepped up and said, 'No worries, we've got this.'

"They had a massive spacejet all ready in the desert with a brand new ion drive. They blasted farther out into the Solar System than anybody before, caught the space rock and stayed there. Hid out on the rings of Neptune for a couple of years.

"They came back with the Peter Foundation Graviton Device. They could equip any celestial body – planet, moon, asteroid, whatever – with any level of gravity they wanted. It's insanely expensive, and they won't tell anybody how it works, and now we can't live without the things. They installed one on the Moon and figured out how to manufacture an atmosphere that stuck around. Now their tech is everywhere. They basically made colonization possible."

Simon nodded. "Yep, yep. So you know what everybody knows. All right, so how did they pull it off? Tell me that."

Joe shrugged. "Like I said, nobody knows. They made some kind of device from the space rock. Nobody has any idea even what it looks like, security around the Foundation Devices is so tight. Every planet other than Earth has one. Somehow it links up to the center of the planet and gives the planet gravity."

Simon nodded again. "Yeah. Most closely guarded secret in the Galaxy. But I know a guy who knows a guy." He beamed with pride, then all happiness fell off his face. "Now. Show me that wedge again."

Joe held it up in front of the screen. "You got a light, like a flash or something?" Joe hunted around the apartment and pulled one out of a drawer. "Okay, now shine it at the side of the wedge. Kind of slanty-like."

Joe turned the beam of light almost edgewise to one side of the wedge. Both he and Simon looked at it. A dull, black sheen and nothing else. "Okay, rotate it one more. Do the next side." Joe rotated it in his fingers.

The beam of light struck the next side. Ghostly letters and numbers flowed into view, hovering a half inch above the wedge. "Trippy," Joe muttered.

"Yeah, fancy laser etching, only activates in certain light. Okay, hold that there." The string of numbers and letters meant nothing to Joe. Simon peered up at them and down at something in his lap. Up and down, up and down.

"Okay, got it," he said. "So, the Foundation Graviton Device basically has two parts. Part one is the device. That's what they stick on the planet, or moon, or whatever, right up the south pole. It lets the Foundation engineers customize the gravity field. You want to make a town heavier, so its water systems drain better or something? Want a city to be lighter, like your Canal City over there? Or just uniform Earth-normal everywhere? The device makes it happen, don't ask me how.

"Part two is the Graviton. A small, black wedge about six inches long. It's the power source that makes the whole gravity thing work. Every Graviton looks the same, but they're all different. The Foundation brains found a way to tweak them somehow to give the right amount of juice. Are you getting me, Mr. Drive? You're holding a piece of that space rock. That there is a Graviton."

It seemed to get a little heavier in Joe's hand, like it was proud of the recognition. "All right," he said, holding it a bit farther away. "So, we have anything to worry about here?"

Simon gave him a look. "Each wedge is different," he continued, "custom made for every application. They're always the same size, but different strengths. Then the Device takes that raw gravity and shapes it for whatever we need. Look at the etching again."

Joe angled the light until the numbers jumped off the side of the black rock. "See how that string starts with an M?" Joe nodded. "This one's specifically for the Moon. Those numbers after it?" Simon pointed to a long string of digits that meant nothing to Joe. "They don't add up."

"What do you mean?" Joe said.

"I mean, they tell you how strong the thing is. What kind of gravity it's going to produce. And what you're holding there doesn't jive with what the Moon needs."

"Really," Joe said. "Less or more?"

Simon stared doom through the screen. "More, man. A lot more."

Joe thought about that. "You mean, like, if they slip this

thing in instead of the one that's already there, I weigh 300 pounds?" Simon shook his head. "400?"

"More."

"What, like 500 pounds?"

"More, man. Listen, I'm no expert. The Device shapes the gravity force this thing puts out, right? But if I'm reading those numbers properly, what you've got there holds enough power to flatten whatever it's focused on."

"Say that again," Joe said. He tried to imagine it, and couldn't.

"You heard me. Pick a spot on the Moon, and say goodbye to every building, every person, every everything. Flat. Or dial it up and kill the entire Moon."

"Wait, what?!" Joe leaned back from the link, an instinctive move.

"Yeah. So. I don't know what you're doing over there on the Red Planet, but promise me one thing, Joe."

"What's that?"

"Promise me that weirdo killer wedge never, ever comes home with you. Don't ever let it get closer to the Moon than it is right now."

It had been awhile since he'd taken a breath. Joe forced himself to suck one in. "You're serious about all this."

"Oh yeah. And you'd better be, too. Whoever lost that thing is going to want it back. We seriously don't want to let them have it."

"All right," Joe said, "you got yourself a promise. Gotta go."

Simon leaned in close. "Wipe your link, man. This conversation never happened." The screen went blank.

Joe tucked the wedge away and spent a couple of minutes wiping out his link's memory, rebuilding it from scratch. Then he got ready for his next meeting with Miles.

Chapter 15

Joe considered reusing the Fong disguise for his trip back to the Red Zone, or perhaps the geeky kid disguise Kate had given him. Too late for that, though. By this time everyone who was anyone knew that Joe Drive was back on Mars. He strode away from Kate's safe house with his own face, feeling distinctly naked.

The casino hotel was hopping. Several second-rate conventions had filled the place to the brim with eager casino bait. Joe saw bright nametags shimmering above hundreds of heads as attendees swirled through the lobby and crammed the lifts. He swam upstream to his room, took an hour to brace himself, then headed for the casino floor.

It was jammed. The vids and race screen parlors were wall to wall with conventioneers, threaded through by servers, security, and at least three opportunistic entrepreneurs with sticky fingers. He sat at the bar watching the fun for a few minutes, then moved to the tables. The games that required a level of attention or commitment still had seats available.

Two minutes after he sat down at blackjack a server

brushed past and dropped a drink by his elbow. "Compliments of the house, Mr. Drive," he murmured and was gone. The slim flute contained a purple liquid with a thin, wavering streak of crimson hot sauce dropped through the middle. Joe smiled at it, then lifted the glass and tipped a salute towards the nearest security camera. He sipped. It was an Ion Burn, distilled from the fields of mineral ice on the poles of Io.

Someone remembered Captain Joe Drive's taste in liquor.

Altogether, it was a well-executed little message from the casino management. No disguise needed. Welcome back and enjoy the hospitality. Stay out of trouble.

He'd actually made a small pile by the time Miles arrived. Despite the milling throng, Joe caught the ripple. A security camera swivelled on its mount. A server put down a loaded drinks tray and left it unattended as she hustled to take up a position along a wall. Several patrons, including one badly-dressed mingler Joe had pegged as a lightfinger, perked up and paid attention. A moment later Miles slid onto the stool two down from Joe.

That was more than a ripple, Joe thought. And Miles looks stressed.

They ignored each other as Miles placed the three bets – seven, six, nine this time. He was fidgeting, not giving much attention to the cards, playing around with his other chips. Joe saw the shifting pattern of chips on the velvet briefly form the letter H, then Miles swept them back into a sloppy pile.

It was their old code. H for Hot. No kidding, old friend, he thought. As Miles left, the increased surveillance in the room seemed to settle down. None of it redirected onto Joe, as far as he could tell.

After another ten minutes – and after finishing his excellent drink – Joe cashed in and made his way out of the casino.

Even the hallways were full of conventioneers, by this time well into their party. He pushed through to suite 769 and knocked on the door. Miles cracked the door to let him in and pushed it closed again to shut out the noise.

He'd found his smile, albeit a little strained. "Exploding novas, my friend, but you've set me to a job. This little venture of yours has stirred up the ant's nest. They're trying to crawl all over me just for being near you. But hey," he shrugged and laughed, "things were getting boring around here."

His humor returned like a sun rising through storm clouds. Miles waved at the door. "Did you see all those fresh faces?" he said, ushering Joe into a sumptuously overdecorated living room. "If it wasn't for this little errand of yours I'd be hip deep in new prospects by now. I know we're friends, but if there's any profit in this little venture, feel free to throw some shine my way."

"Oh. Yeah. Not a problem." Joe had barely touched Ella's expense allowance, not to mention the assassin's attempt at a bribe. He flipped out his wallet and flashed some of it over to Miles.

Miles smiled his thanks, then looked again and whistled. "Brilliant. Now let's see what you've bought." He gestured to a small side table. A holo generator waited to be turned on. "I must say, mate, I had to do some fancy dancing for this little prize. But here you go." He pressed an indent on the side of the holo.

Images and data screens flared into life above the table. Joe saw Ella, Wheeler and her two brothers in numerous publicity stills and paparazzi shots, entertaining Elites at one of their mansions or playing in the Poundville countryside. News reels and financial reports flickered by. Joe stopped and expanded a few of them, but he'd mostly uncovered the same intel in his own searches.

"Wait for it," Miles murmured as he saw disappointment on Joe's face.

After two minutes of mediocre intel, the data screens faded away and left one large, 3D image hovering in the air. Joe whistled. "Is that what I think it is?"

"You're welcome. Now, if there's nothing else?"

"No, no, this should do it. Thanks Miles, I'll be in touch. Go play." Joe kept his eyes on the prize for another minute, then thumbed it off and picked up the holo generator. By the time he had it in his pocket Miles was gone.

He pushed through the crowds to his own room, turned the thing back on and studied the security layout for the Pound family asteroid.

How the hell had Miles laid his paws on this? A luminescent globe hovered above the holo generator, speckled with swaths of green grasslands and forest, areas of grey towns, and small dots of blue that must be lakes. Thin, wavering lines crisscrossed the air around Poundville, changing every few seconds. Bright pinpoints glowed at regular intervals over the entire surface of the clear, ghostly ball.

He stuck out his hands, grabbed the edges of the holo and pulled. The entire construct expanded, revealing tiny notes and timetables attached to the image. He pulled up a chair and got to work.

Poundville was roundish, not completely spherical, like most asteroids its size. Five mansions sat at roughly equidistant points across the surface. The largest – Wheeler's place, Joe guessed – occupied the center of a sizeable town. The others had settlements nearby for support workers, but nothing as grand as the main house. A few small lakes filled in low spots on the landscape. The rest of it was various shades of green, denoting grassland and a small forest.

The bright lights were security bases. Nine of them in total, some located close to the mansions and the rest peppering the surface of Poundville, providing a security blanket over the entire asteroid. Alongside each base were charts detailing troop numbers and patrol times. Joe filed these away in the back of his mind.

The wavy lines in the air above the asteroid were flight paths. Air patrols, constant and ever-changing. The paths altered with every flight, the times adjusted randomly, so that the lines seemed to flicker and move over the asteroid.

Around it all, only visible at this magnification, a thin shell enclosed everything. A note attached to the shell said Communications and Surveillance Screen.

Joe leaned back in his chair. This was why Ella had sought him out, him and no other. Poundville was unapproachable. Nobody got close to the asteroid undetected, and no communications got in or out. Ella must have been able to piggyback on some authorized signal for her transmissions.

"Can you do it?" Ella stood three feet behind his right shoulder, her feet not denting the plush carpet. She watched him watch the spinning planetoid. Deep sadness was etched across her face. Now that Joe knew her predicament and her wish to help the rebels at any cost, he understood.

If he couldn't crack this, her grand plan failed. If he did, she was dead. Damned if you do, damned if you don't.

"Jesus, lady, would you please knock or something? And give me a chance, I only just got this." She was dressed in everyday casual again, billowy white shirt and loose breeches. House arrest clothes. He pointed to one of the mansions, the one in the southern hemisphere farthest away from the big one. "This is you?"

She nodded. "I have one lifebot with me at all times, and

a small guard contingent on the grounds. I hope you can figure this out, Joe, you're the only one who can. Please try. Please hurry." Her image shimmered and faded, then stabilized.

"Listen, Ella. I haven't – I mean, isn't there any other way? Talk to a lawyer, talk to your father, something? I know you mean well, and sure, the rebels could use the help, but this crazy plan. I just," he searched for the words and came up empty. "I just don't know."

"I'm not getting out of here." She waved a hand at the holo. "Surely you can see that. The Resistance is losing, Joe, and without the Endowment's help they have no way to fight back. Most of the rebels have pulled back to the Moon and Venus already." Her sadness hardened into conviction. "You have to do this, Joe. I insist."

"Wait. Wait, did you say the Moon? That's a rebel stronghold?" Ella's form shimmered and thinned. She lifted a hand to him, almost touching. Then she was gone.

Joe sat in the quiet of his room, lit by the glow from the swirling holographic asteroid. At last he turned back to it. "Okay, Drive," he murmured, "the lady says you're the one. Let's see how good you are."

He had the security base technical data. He had the patrol flight times. He was sure Kate could find him a small, fast spacejet. If he asked nice. He settled in to study.

And in thirty minutes he had it. He reached out a finger, jabbed it into a tiny blank space over Poundville and stopped the shimmering security measures. "Got you," he whispered into the dark.

Chapter 16

It was late, and Joe had had a long day. Still, he knew better than to spend the night in the Red Zone hotel. All of Mars knew he was here. He felt distinctly exposed.

Joe was halfway through the Red Zone's capacious lobby, feeling the first nervous sweat between his shoulder blades at the thought of using the hotel's transpo booth, when he spotted the hood of a grey cloak over the top of a lounge chair. Ryza peeked up over the top of the chair, raised a hand and beckoned him over. Half amused, half curious, and ashamedly relieved for the delay in getting to the transpo booth, Joe altered course and joined him in the next chair.

"Fancy meeting you here," he said, "although I expect it's no accident."

The monk laughed. He seemed delighted to see Joe again. "No, probably not. Pull that thing over." Their chairs were part of a loose collection in the middle of the lobby, so no one noticed as Joe yanked his around to face Ryza. The monk considered the placement, pulled his own chair up so they were face to face with knees almost touching again, and seemed satisfied. He pulled a small black box out from his robe and put it on the arm of his chair.

Joe heard the noise of the lobby around them descend into a soft murmur. "There," said Ryza. "Now we don't have to yell at each other and no one else can hear us." He noticed Joe's look of surprise and added, "It's only a sound blanket generator. Simple stuff. So, let's get down to it. You've had a busy couple of days, Joe. Nice job at the tables tonight, by the way, your winnings will almost pay for this trip."

"I didn't see you there." He was starting to think he couldn't fart on this dessicated red rock without it making the news reels.

Ryza laughed again. He'd pulled his hood down, revealing that youthful face and close-cropped blond haircut Joe remembered from Heaviside. The kid's blue eyes were bright with intelligence and, as Joe saw now, a burning curiosity. The kind of flame that could lead a young man into trouble. But Joe found himself liking the monk.

"We're trained to observe from the sidelines and interfere as little as possible. I've been watching you go all over the place, Joe. You've met a few people. Your friend from the casino looks like fun. He gave you a little something tonight. Mind if I ask what it is?"

Joe gave his own little laugh. "You can ask."

Ryza shrugged. "No doubt something to make it easier for you to get up there." He gestured towards the ceiling, and Poundville beyond. Then those bright eyes glittered. "Want to tell me how you plan on breaking the security? Maybe I could come along for the ride."

"Not a chance, monk. That's my business, not yours."

Ryza sank back into his chair, disappointed. "You're not going to make this easy, are you? Let me ask you this: has this small job, whatever it is, attracted more heat than it should? You've been in a scrape or two already, if I'm not mistaken. In your professional opinion, are the bad guys overreacting a bit?"

He was mirroring Joe's own thoughts. "Maybe. Yeah."

The monk lifted a hand out of his robe and pointed at Joe's chest. "There you go. Pay attention to the signs. This adventure might not be as little as it seems. You might appreciate some company before it's done."

The kid's argument held enough weight to make Joe reconsider, but he still came to the same conclusion. "No," he answered at last. "However I get up there, you can't hitch a ride." He rose to go.

"One last thing," Ryza stopped him with a hand on his knee. That glitter was back in his eyes. "Have you found anything lately? Not whatever your sly friend slipped you tonight, but something else? Maybe something unusual or strange?"

Joe thought about it. Why not? It was the Foundation's thing, after all. "Yeah. I came into possession of this." He fiddled around for a moment and held out his hand, clenched fist facing down. Ryza reached out and he dropped the black wedge into the monk's outstretched hand.

Copying Joe's stealth, Ryza wrapped his fingers over the object and drew it into the folds of his cloak. Then he unfurled his fingers and looked down. Instantly, the color drained from the kid's face. He turned it on edge, catching the light to read the faint numbers etched into its side. "Where did you get this?" he whispered.

Joe told him. Elite assassin, Joe came out on top. The man without a name dropped off the edge of a cliff, leaving behind the wedge and a host of questions. Simon's intel about the wedge's true nature, which Ryza didn't need to hear. He'd been studying the numbers on the wedge's side as Joe talked and his cheeks were now burning red with anger.

"So that's all I know. You're welcome to keep it. Just make sure it never gets back to the Moon."

Ryza was silent for a long time. Joe let him mull over the new intel and scanned the hotel lobby. Another convention of Elites had arrived from Earth. He saw a flotilla of brightly-clad gamblers pour out of the line of buzzing and crackling transpo booths and flow towards the waiting clerks, some of them jumping up and down, delighted with the forgiving shift in gravity.

The monk's sound blanket seemed to be working. No one on the floor was interested in the muffled conversation happening in the middle of the lobby. But he saw three surveillance cameras pointed their way, and as he watched a fourth began to swivel.

"We're attracting some interest," he muttered to Ryza.

That snapped the monk out of his reverie. He gave the wedge one more look of extreme distaste and handed it back, making sure no one saw. "Keep it," he said. "Tuck it away again and don't show it to anybody else. For whatever reason, this device has come to you, and you need to hang onto it. Keep it safe, Joe."

Joe took it, puzzled, and put it back in its hiding place. "I thought this was your field of expertise. The Peter Foundation makes these, right? I figured you'd want it back."

Ryza leaned forward again, all trace of humor gone. "Follow that thought, Joe. The Peter Foundation makes Graviton wedges, yes. We're the only ones who can. Each wedge is custom manufactured for one purpose, one location." The blush of anger in his face deepened. "That wedge's purpose? I – I can't even – it's unimaginable, Joe. An abomination."

"You don't know who to trust."

The monk nodded. "Keep it safe. I'll see you again

soon." He grabbed his sound blanket, stood and hustled for a transpo booth. The noise of the hotel lobby crashed over Joe like a wave. He sat for another minute, steeling himself, then headed for the line of booths.

Chapter 17

Three random stops later he emerged a block from Kate's safe house. Nobody followed. He got inside without incident, locked the place down and went gratefully to bed.

A soft but insistent chime pulled him up from a deep sleep sometime in the small hours of the night. "What?" he grumbled into the dark.

"Intrusion attempt detected," answered a disembodied, vaguely feminine voice. So much for his stealth moves. "Four people. Two at the entrance, two standing a slight distance away. All armed." A moment later, as Joe was yanking on his pants, a muffled thud came from the main room. The sound of a punched-out lock mechanism hitting the carpet. "Intrusion successful."

Four attackers. Two to breach by blowing the lock, two to guard. Joe knew the pattern. He'd done it a dozen times, trained for it fifty more. "Fast and quiet!" Garfield had drilled it into them. "Catch the Lowlifes before they know what's hit 'em."

An Interstellar Space Force squad had just broken through his door. He flipped the Sunfire out of its holster and knelt by the bed.

The bedroom door stayed closed. No further sounds came to his ears. "Where are they?" he muttered, maintaining his crouch.

A nondescript bulge in the middle of the bedroom ceiling dropped an inch to reveal a row of lenses, glowed to life and sent thin, greenish beams of light towards the far wall. The wall lit up with a ghostly, line-sketch hologram of the living room on the other side. He saw the outlines of the sofa and dining table, some chairs, and the entrance to the kitchen. Three pale, badly-rendered figures moved about the main room. The fourth, keeping still with a gun at the ready, had his back against the wall right next to the bedroom door. Waiting for Joe.

He glanced up at the ceiling. Wild tech. But considering who owned the place, he shouldn't have been surprised.

The squad was looking for something. The three searchers methodically went over every inch of the apartment, omitting nothing. Joe could hear the shuffles and bumps as they looked behind books, inside drawers, under carpets.

"Remember, black wedge, about six inches long, could be anywhere," he heard one of them murmur. They seemed to know that Joe was in the bedroom, and seemed content to leave him there. The search was the priority.

Until, a minute later, they finished tossing the place and came up empty. Then they all converged on the bedroom door. "Here we go," Joe muttered, and made the Sunfire comfortable in his hand.

They spread out, weapons raised, to cover the door. One of them spoke up. "Captain Drive," he called, just loud enough to be heard through the wall. "We know you're awake. Open the door and surrender your weapon and you will not be harmed."

"Oh yeah?" he called back. "What about my dignity?"

The sketchy figure doing the talking actually smiled. "That can't be helped, sir. But I have orders direct from Commander Garfield to deliver you unharmed. If possible." Right on cue, all four of them took a step closer to the door and away from a direct line of fire. Standard operating procedure.

He ran the numbers. Four assailants. Same training as him. The apartment's hologram trick gave him an edge. He could get one of them through the wall. Maybe two, if they were startled by the first shot, but that was unlikely. Then the fun would begin in earnest.

And he would lose. At least his gun arm, if they were really good marksmen, burned off at the elbow. Probably a whole lot more than that.

Joe had enjoyed his three years of freedom. He hadn't known until this moment how much. Being taken captive would feel lousy. Still, it beat being dead.

Except for the other thing. They had orders to present him like a chicken dinner to Commander Blinken Garfield. Trussed up in restrictor cuffs. Maybe in chains. That scorched any thought of surrender under a hot, burning anger.

He swung the Sunfire over to the target on the far left. Might as well try for a clean sweep. The soldier on the right reached for the panel and the bedroom door swished open.

He fired at the wall. The Sunfire warmed as laser fire erupted throughout the room. His beam tore through the wall and caught the hologram figure on the other side amidships, doubling him over with a shriek. A flash of heat roared through the bed above him as one soldier tried a shot from the door.

Then the holograms, one of them now an actual man in the door, sprouted red crosshair reticles at each center mass. The bump in the middle of the ceiling began a high and rising whine as more of its lenses pivoted into targeting mode.

Joe had enough reflexes to duck and cover his eyes. The apartment exploded with lightning and thunder . The crackle of burning ozone and bad barbecue filled the air. Then – silence.

"Intrusion liquidated," said the vaguely female voice. "Cleaning service notified."

Joe stood up. Leftover adrenaline – and a little fear of the safe house – made him shaky on his legs. He placed the Sunfire carefully on the night table. Air scrubbers had whirred into life and were busy pulling smoke out of the room.

The bedroom was a disaster. Half the bed was burned through, smoke curling up from the remainder of the sheets. The far wall had three large holes punched through it, plus the small one made by the Sunfire. There was practically no wall left, to speak of. In the doorway, from where the one soldier had scorched a path through the bed, was a smouldering, sticky mass of disassembled human. He maneuvered around it and found three more in the living room. The carnage was incredible. He'd never seen anything like it.

His link buzzed. It was Kate. "You all right?" she asked when he accepted the call. "I forgot to tell you, the place has a security system. It pings me when it's been activated."

"Security system?" He found a clean spot on the sofa and lowered himself onto it. "Thing packs more firepower than an orbital railgun. Yeah, I'm fine."

"That's good. The cleaners are on their way, so sit tight. Any idea who they were?"

"Garfield's team." The words burned acid through his gut. "They had two objectives. The first was to bring me in. To Garfield directly. The second was to find something. They tossed the place."

"Garfield? He's wrapped up in this? That's interesting. Any idea what they were looking for?"

"Not a clue," he lied. "Whatever it was, they didn't find it. And even if they did, they're not in any shape to deliver."

"Hmm. You do realize you've cost me my safe house." She sounded matter-of-fact about it.

"Yeah, sorry about that. Blame it on Garfield."

"I just might. Well, hang tight, Joe. I'll be over in a bit."

The kitchen and liquor cabinet were unscathed. He made himself an Ion Burn and went back to the couch. His ears rang with the silence. His thoughts raced around in circles, picking up pieces of this crazy, insane day and reorienting them into a new reality.

The squad – what was left of them – was dressed all in black. Joe could see no insignia, nothing that marked them as Interstellar Space Force soldiers. They had come here for him, but he hadn't been their prime objective. They'd only tried the bedroom once their search failed to find the black wedge. Which meant that the wedge was a more important objective than Joe.

Garfield had sent them to get the wedge. Commander Blinken Garfield knew about the wedge. Did he know what it was? What it could do? Or was he just following someone else's orders?

Joe dismissed the question after a single second. Garfield made it his business to know everything. He knew what the black wedge was. And he suspected that Joe possessed it. So he knew about the assassin on the Moon.

In a leap he wouldn't have believed possible, Joe found himself hating Garfield more than he had five minutes before. The man was nothing less than a monster.

The intercom buzzed. Three men and a woman, loaded down with supplies and actually dressed like housekeepers, stared into the viewscreen. "Cleaners," the woman said. He let them in.

They went to work without a word to him or each other, obviously well-practiced. Two of them took care of the biologic mess while the others set about rebuilding the apartment with quick studs, instant wall and repair compound.

Partway through their work Kate arrived. She looked around. The woman cleaner spared a moment to nod a silent greeting and they spent a minute in a quiet huddle, discussing the situation. Joe got the impression they'd done this before. Then Kate ushered him into the kitchen.

"You all right?" she asked him again. She glanced at the drink in his hand, now almost gone.

"Yeah. Not happy, though. Sorry about the place, Kate, but you can send Garfield the bill. This was his crew. They said as much."

"Count on it," Kate muttered, looking around. "What were they looking for?"

"Never got a chance to ask them," he said, skirting around the answer. Kate zeroed in on his eyes and stared at him for a moment.

"Never were a good liar, Drive. Promise me you'll tell me what this was all about sometime. You owe me that."

"No idea what you're talking about," he said, but made the small hand sign for affirmative. She caught the gesture and nodded.

"So. Did Miles come through?"

Miles Crookshanks. The meeting with his old friend seemed like a long time ago. He fished out the holo generator, miraculously undamaged. "Yeah, he did. I don't know how, but he managed to find this." He placed the holo on the kitchen table, flicked it on, and Poundville's security layout blossomed in the air between them.

Kate glanced at it. She frowned, then glared at him. "This is what you were looking for?"

He pointed to the spinning globe. "Well, not this, exactly. I asked him for anything he could get, and he came back with this. Pretty impressive, if you ask me. It's exactly what I need."

She sighed. "I suppose there's no way you could have known."

"Known what?"

"Joe. I'm a security expert. On Mars. In Canal City. Right below Poundville." She waited for him to get it.

He groaned, then waved his hand through the middle of the holo. "This is yours?"

"I designed Poundville's security protocols, soup to nuts." She examined the holo closely for a moment, then grabbed it and zoomed in until they had disappeared under the surface of the asteroid, right to the middle of the sphere. Hanging in the exact center of the display was the York Security Consultancy logo. "If I'd known you wanted to infiltrate Poundville, I could have simply told you to forget it. There's no way."

He leaned back. "Really. The arrangements are good, I'll give you that. Practically airtight. But I found a way to get to her."

Kate shook her head. "No you didn't."

Now it was his turn to frown. "Yeah, I did. Gimme five." He flipped his wallet and five credits hovered in the air between them.

The ghost of a smile came back to her face, a welcome sight. "All right." Her five joined his. "First question. Who gave you this?"

"Miles, of course. And he had to work hard for it. He was nervous as hell when he gave it to me."

Her smile grew a notch. "Exactly. So, tell me. When have you ever known Miles Crookshanks to work hard?"

"Hey now, that's my friend ... oh." He glowered at the holo again. "You think so?"

"Let's find out."

She spent five minutes poring over the security arrangements, zooming in and out on schedules, rosters, flight paths. At the end of it, she jabbed a finger into the puzzle and stopped the flow of screens and images on a single flight roster. "There! That's the vulnerability you discovered?"

He examined it. "That's the one. On this rotation, twice a day, the patrol flights miss five square kilometres of airspace right over the southern mansion. Drop in, do the job, lift out. Done."

She gave him an appreciative thumbs-up. "Good eye. That's almost impossible to see, and you found the flaw. Keep the five, you earned it. However," she added, "good thing you wanted me to double-check Miles' intel first. Because this gap doesn't exist."

"They got to Miles," he growled. Kate laughed.

"Got to Miles? All it would take was a bigger payday. How much did you offer him?"

"Um. He did it as a favor. I tossed him a little as a tip."

She laughed again, harder. "Didn't take much, then. If you'd found a ship and flown into that hole, the ISF would have blown you to bits."

"I guess." He started. "Wait, what? The ISF?" He gestured at the patrol lines and personnel rosters. "I thought these were private contractors."

Kate shook her head. "Hardly. I put the plan together, but it's the Interstellar Space Force who maintain security on Poundville. Ground to orbit, it's all military."

For the second time in as many hours Joe sat down because he needed to. The ISF had been created by the Home Alliance government on Earth and charged with the defence of humanity. In recent years they'd been tasked with controlling rebel incursions, which at least could be justified in the name of planetary peace.

But guard duty? For an individual family?

The last of the Ion Burn tasted foul in his mouth. "Wheeler Pound owns the ISF."

Kate squinted and waggled a hand. "Not really. The Home Alliance commands the Interstellar Space Force. But Wheeler Pound and the Home Alliance are partners. Home Alliance governs Earth, and they've authorized Wheeler Pound to run everything else. He directs the ISF off Earth, with Home Alliance's permission." She shrugged. "It pretty much adds up to the same thing. So, yeah."

"Wait, wait." It was too late in the evening for this. A hurricane was blowing through his mind, everything thrown into the air and twisting. He strode out of the kitchen and back into the apartment's main room. The cleaning crew, sensing the mood, paused in their work and stood back.

One of the human puddles still stained the floor. He walked over to it. Bits of black clothing, hardly even a uniform. Regulation boots – no soldier could get away from a good pair of boots, Joe still had a set in his closet back on the Moon. These were Garfield's men, incognito and off the books.

What books? They weren't working for the Interstellar Space Force. They were Wheeler Pound's men. Garfield was waiting for them to escort him back to Poundville.

So Garfield himself was Wheeler Pound's man.

Joe walked over to the scorched and blackened wall, already half-repaired. Garfield had been looking for the black wedge. Did that mean that Wheeler Pound knew about it as well? He shook his head, forcing more pieces to fall into place. How completely was Wheeler running Garfield? Had Wheeler told Garfield to come and find it?

Joe knew what the wedge could do. Its only purpose was to crush someplace on the Moon. No one would survive. Not rebels, not Elites, not anybody. Garfield knew that, Joe was certain. Did Wheeler?

Who had commissioned the evil thing? Only a senior scientist in the Peter Foundation could have made it. Had Wheeler given the order? According to Kate's revelation, he had the clout. Wheeler Pound, it seemed, ran everything off-Earth. He could order the Moon's gravity changed.

And gravity doesn't lie, Joe thought. Gravity was like the truth. There was no running away from it.

The place smelled terrible. He turned back to the kitchen and paused at the doorway as one more piece fell into place with a thud. "She's not going to like that," he said, then went back to the holo generator and its spinning, useless model of Poundville.

"Like what?" came Kate's voice from behind him.

"Nothing. So, that hole in the Poundville patrols doesn't exist. Tell me, is there any way in? And out again?"

Kate shook her head. "No. You'll get detected a hundred miles out, and most likely burned out of the sky before you ever get to the surface. Even a direct order from me wouldn't stop it."

He knew it was true. He'd examined the plans himself. "Doesn't matter," he growled. "I'm getting up there. Wheeler Pound has some questions to answer. And there's Garfield."

Kate broke into a full-on smile. She reached out and patted him on the cheek. "I know that look. Takes you awhile to break orbit, Drive, but once you get up to speed you're unstoppable. Of course you're getting there. Can't wait to see how you figure it out."

He reached out and spun the Poundville holo. Yeah. He couldn't wait to see, either. Somehow he was getting up there. The whole situation, from Daddy Wheeler's megalomaniac politics to the ISF's corruption to Ella's hopeless plea, stank as badly as the safe house. Joe wanted answers, and he was going to get them.

He was going to Poundville. And when he left the miserable, pretentious little asteroid he wouldn't be alone. Ella Pound would be with him. She needed to live. She needed to be free. Joe saw it now. Ella Pound had a job to do, maybe the most important job in the entire Solar System.

And she'd been right after all. Joe Drive was the only one who could pull it off.

Chapter 18

When the cleaners had finished their work the apartment smelled like a cross between a construction site and a laboratory clean room, but all trace of the slaughter was gone. Joe briefly considered heading back to the Red Zone to get some sleep but decided to stay put. Kate's apartment was still probably the safest place on Mars.

He closed the door behind the crew, made another drink and stood in the dark by the living room window. Canal City glowed with the lights of the casinos. Dawn was only a couple of hours away. The place was as quiet as it ever got, just a muted hum of city machinery filtering in through the night.

Deimos and Phobos were both in the sky tonight. Poundville hung there, too, maybe a third the size of the Earth's full moon, the same size as Phobos but in an orbit ten times further out. The surface of Poundville glowed green with terraformed grasslands and forest, a few glittering lights marking the Pound family mansions and towns. Beyond them all he could make out the tiny blue dot of Earth. Where humans had first begun. Where they had populated and depleted an entire planet, then reached out to colonize and start depleting all the rest.

Where this whole mess had started.

Poundville winked at him as a Martian cloud breezed across the sky. Ella was up there. Deep inside the South Mansion, kept there by a father who didn't like to be disobeyed. Determined to die because it was the only way she could think of to get out from under his clutches and help humanity. So determined, and – as Joe knew now – so wrong.

He sipped the Ion Burn and toasted her, up on that suspended marble. He would give her that chance to make a difference. She deserved it. For all the good it would do. The forces of colonization and industry were strong, and had almost a century of momentum behind them. Joe knew how pitiless and relentless they could be. He'd once been the tip of their spear.

Echoes of his last ISF flight came to him out of the stillness of the night. The hiss of the precision bombs, targeted to a small handful of rebel commanders in the village below the clouds, falling through the Martian atmosphere. The rough growl of his spacejet's wings as he dropped almost to ground level to get below the clouds. The thunder as his bombs, so much larger than he'd programmed, powdered whole neighborhoods of red-earth houses as they ate the entire Lowlife village.

The screams, reaching him even through the canopy of his spacejet. Reaching him again in the dark of the night three years later.

Joe sighed, tossed off the last of his drink and headed for the freshly-rebuilt bedroom. He'd find his way to Poundville. He had questions for old man Pound, and Blinken Garfield was up there somewhere. He would right some wrongs and help Ella help humanity. But he wasn't at all certain it would be enough.

It wasn't his night for sleep. Ten minutes after he'd closed his eyes he leaped off the bed again, Sunfire in his hand. "Oh. It's you," he grumbled.

Ella looked worried. "What did you do, Joe?" she asked. She was seated at what must be her console, hands busy and eyes everywhere but on him. "The soldiers are all nervous and excited here. The communications screen has tightened, I can barely see you. They've changed up their patrols. My father has tried to call me three times. Was that you?"

"What did your dad have to say?" He got up and began to dress. Ella didn't even notice.

"Father? Pfft. I don't talk to him. Not since he threw me down here. Not since I discovered what he really is. What have you done, Joe?"

He grimaced. "Nothing. Garfield sent a welcoming committee and I sent them away. That's all."

Now she did look at him. Hard. Then nodded. "Good. I'm glad you're back up to your potential, Captain Drive. Now, will you help? When will you come?"

She sounded so fixed on self destruction, almost eager for it. Even though he knew why, it chilled him. "Knock it off, Ella. I'm not going to kill you, just forget it. Wouldn't work, anyway, not the way you think it would."

Her determination morphed once more into desperation. "But you have to! And it will! I had the best lawyers look over my will, it's ironclad. All my money will go to the Endowment, and from there to the Resistance. Once I'm – dead."

"Oh, really. The best lawyers." He'd been shot at, nearly taken captive, and lied to by a friend. His anger was close to the surface now, and it gave his words an edge. "You didn't tell me that your father is working with the Home Alliance. Practically partners with them. That he tells the ISF in these parts what to do. That seems to have slipped your mind."

"Slipped my mind?" Now she was confused, he could see it in her face. "What do you mean? That would be like standing in the desert and pointing out the sand. Of course my father calls the shots off Earth. He's Wheeler Pound. Everyone knows that."

Had Joe been that out of touch? "Well, maybe. So your lawyers told you what the law says about your will, right? What do you think Daddy Pound will do when he sees a sizeable chunk of his wealth poised to go to the rebels?"

Her confusion deepened, then he saw the moment the truth landed.

"Yeah, that's right, Ella. Your father owns the politicians. The lawmakers do what he tells them to. He'll simply rewrite the law."

If she hadn't been sitting at her console she would have fallen down. He saw the color drain from her face. "I've been so stupid," she murmured. "He'll win. He always wins. No matter how rich the Endowment gets, no matter how much I fundraise or donate, it doesn't matter. He always wins. He always ..." Her voice slipped into an indistinct mutter.

Joe sat up straight on the side of his bed. "Take it easy, Ella," he said. "I'm coming up there regardless. Don't know how yet, but I'm coming. And listen, I've – "

She faded, then shimmered. He saw her hands fly around off-screen. "Joe? I'm losing you. I'm – oh no, he's – " And she was gone.

In her place was another hologram. What, was his address scrawled on a bathroom wall somewhere? An older man stood before him, slender like Ella, but somehow sharper. It was the nose, he decided, thin and knife-edged.

Joe was looking at Wheeler Pound. Undeclared dictator of the Solar System. Behind the old man's ice-pale eyes, Joe thought Pound looked tired. And sad.

The image stabilized. Wheeler Pound seemed to see him. Those two blue eyes locked on to his. "Joseph Drive?" Wheeler's voice carried a command presence, but it was tinged with something else. "You are Captain Drive?"

"Not Captain, just Joe. Hello, Mr. Pound. To what do I owe the pleasure?"

"You know who I am, good. That will save some time for us, I think. Tell me, Joe. You have been in contact with my daughter, Ella? She has been speaking with you?"

Pound had intercepted Ella's holo stream. He already knew the answer. "Yeah, she called me. We've talked a couple of times."

It was the middle of the night, even on Poundville. Wheeler had thrown on a shirt, but his thick wave of dark hair was mussed. Joe guessed that they'd alerted him when Ella started transmitting. Now the sadness Joe had glimpsed in the man's face edged closer to the surface.

"What did she say? How is she?" he asked, and meant every word of it.

Joe was shocked at the honesty he heard in the man's voice. "She's a strong-willed and determined woman, sir. And she's definitely not happy with you."

Relief, amusement and regret flowed across Pound's face in a rush. "No, I suppose she's not. Thank you for telling me this, Mr. Drive. Joe." Pound pursed his lips together in thought, then added, "All right, then. Joe, I pride myself on being a good judge of character. I suspect you are, too. Ella has spoken more with you in the last few days than she has with me in the last year, and Joe, I miss my daughter. I would appreciate having a longer conversation with you. More than I'm comfortable doing over this connection. Earlier this evening I had some people sent to your home." He paused. "Am I to presume I won't be seeing them again?"

Joe remembered the lightning flash of serious laser firepower bouncing off his retinas. "They came for a visit. They're not here anymore."

"Ah." And that was as far as his sympathy went. "Let's see if we can avoid any more unpleasantness. Joe, I am going to send another group. A better one. You see, I would very much like you to come visit me. We need to talk, and I do not travel."

Wheeler put on a trace of a smile and shrugged. We're both apex predators, his body language was saying, let's come to an understanding. Not a bad angle, Joe thought. "I respect those skills of yours, Joe. I do not wish to lose another team. Unfortunately, because you are arguably a hostile enemy and because you have skills, you must come to Poundville under guard. Will you permit that?"

It was Joe's turn. He adopted a look of concern and doubt. "I prefer avoiding unpleasantness, too. And I have a hunch that your invitation isn't one I can refuse. But, Wheeler," he moved in closer to the holo projector, "what assurance do I have that I'll ever leave Poundville once I get there?"

Pound took the implied accusation in stride. Just two apex predators working out the ground rules. "The assurance I can give you, Joe, is my personal guarantee. If you have done your research – and I've been told that you have – then you know that's worth something. But if you insist on fighting the next team then I can't promise anything. They're quite capable.

"I miss my Ella, Joe. We used to have such spirited conversations. Now she won't even answer my calls. Her mind has gone down some dark paths lately, Joe, and haven't been able to talk with her about it. You have. Please consider taking a trip up here."

Pound looked – Joe reached for the word. Real. Like he

was actually worried. Well, shit. "Safe passage up there?" Wheeler nodded. "And then?"

"Whatever you like," Wheeler said. "Back to Canal City, first class. A direct flight back to the Moon if you like. Yes, that would be a fine idea. I just want to talk."

"I want to see Ella. Before we meet, after, it doesn't matter. But I want to see her."

A trace of ice returned to Wheeler's eyes. "That won't be possible."

Joe considered protesting, but sighed. "Okay, we'll talk. You say you sent a team? When will they be here?"

The apartment door chimed and the disembodied voice said, "Four people at the door. One at the panel, three holding back. All heavily armed."

"Thank you, Joe." Wheeler Pound lifted a hand and disappeared from the bedroom.

Joe spent a minute in the semi-dark thinking things over, then signalled the new arrivals to wait another minute and threw together an overnight bag. He spared a grin for the look on Kate's face when she discovered how he'd beaten the unbeatable perimeter security of Poundville. Then he went to the front door.

He triggered the door panel to view mode. Three figures stood a few feet back from the entrance. Right up front, baring his teeth into the viewscreen in a huge, wolfish smile, stood Commander Blinken Garfield.

The Sunfire leaped into Joe's hand as he smacked open the door latch.

Chapter 19

"Joe!" Garfield bellowed when the door slid aside. As if he were greeting an old friend after three years' absence. That was all he got before Joe levelled the Sunfire at his craggy face and pulled the trigger.

Except the Sunfire was in Garfield's hand and Joe's wrist was stinging from the lightning-fast disarm. Garfield popped the charging unit out of the bottom of the laser pistol and slapped the useless item back into Joe's palm. "Great to see you, too," he said, spreading his arms wide. "Come on, cool your jets. Let us in already."

Okay, so it was going to be old school. Garfield's nose had grown an extra bump from when Joe broke it in the officer's mess three years ago. He didn't get it fixed, Joe registered through the haze in his mind. Wears it as a fucking trophy. He dropped the Sunfire and threw his fist at the spot again.

Garfield was fast. Joe's knuckles breezed the tip of his nose as he ducked back. "Whoa!" Garfield laughed, "still a little sore, are we? Pound told me he'd arranged it with you."

"He left out your name," Joe snarled. Where was the apartment security? Why hadn't these four been turned into jelly? Maybe intruders needed to cross the threshold. He stepped back to let the big man in.

Garfield strutted through the door. He was dressed in neck to toe tactical grey, the color of shadows. A black crossed-thrusters pin on his chest and the small twin-Saturns Commander insignia on his shoulder were the only links to the ISF. The other three, none of whom Joe recognized, hung back outside the door and assumed guard positions.

"It's good to see you, boy," Garfield said. His voice grated in Joe's ear. It was the sound of deceit and betrayal. "I always knew you'd be back in the game. Had your little vacation, now you're here on Mars. And an audience with Wheeler Pound!" He laughed again. "Straight to the top. You never did mess around."

Little vacation? Back in the game? The thick, red haze in Joe's brain flared into white-hot rage. He went for the man's throat. Driven by his anger, he almost made it. Garfield blocked, spun and threw Joe to one side with those broad shoulders. Joe recovered and aimed a kick to take out Garfield's knees. The big man danced away.

"Stay out!" Garfield ordered the others, who had moved to intervene. So this was to be one on one. That suited Joe just fine. He leaped to his feet and carried the momentum through to a rib tackle, connecting with Garfield and bringing him down.

He'd tackled a tiger. Garfield got him in the chest, stomach and a shuddering jab across the cheek before flipping over and pinning his arms. "Joe, you've gotten slow," Garfield said, barely even winded. "Calm down and let's go for a flight, Pound's waiting. We'll have plenty of time for combat training later."

It was a good pin. One inch in any direction and his shoulders would scream. Joe roared, locked his shoulders in place and threw his entire body into a spin. Garfield flew off to the side, connecting with a side table and sending an old vase crashing to the floor. Garfield got up, his cheek bleeding from a small cut, and shook his head.

"You always were a slow learner," he said.

They fought. Joe let his reflexes take over, blocking and punching and kicking through the red haze. He felt his knuckles connect, felt his forearms parry incoming blows. Garfield got a good one in and his abdomen imploded with a shriek of pain. Joe fought through it. He cracked a palm strike onto Garfield's face and heard the man grunt. A foot came out of nowhere and connected with his thigh and suddenly Joe had a useless leg. He struck out again, clipped Garfield on the ear. Garfield swore and kept swinging.

Slowly, piece by piece, Joe lost. Another blow to the stomach took his wind. He blocked a roundhouse aimed at his temple and head-butted Garfield on the nose, feeling it crack again. Then another stomach shot almost cost Joe his lunch. He swung and missed. Blocked and missed, and Garfield rattled his temple.

"Give it up, Captain," Garfield said, now breathing hard. Joe aimed for the sound of his voice and hit air. Another shot caught him on the point of the chin and he saw stars.

"You're done," Garfield said. "My orders were to bring you in unharmed. You got a beef with me? Fine. Save it for later."

Joe could see him. Hear him, still giving orders. That hateful voice that had spewed so many lies into Joe's face for so many years. He still had a good leg. He groaned and made as if to relax, to give up. Garfield let down his guard. Took a step forward. Joe straightened his good leg like a caged spring and aimed a knuckle shot at the man's neck, a blow to crush his windpipe and deliver a slow, terrifying death.

"Aw, for hell's sake." Garfield swept aside his attack and Joe felt a meteor crash into his temple. The blackness of interstellar space took him down.

***

The vibration brought him back. It was constant, low, strong, and intimately familiar. He was on the unadorned, unpadded deck of a runabout spacejet that had finished its gravity burn and was accelerating to wherever it was headed next.

The pocket of his shirt had been turned inside out and was tickling his cheek. His other pockets hung loose, too. In the far corner he caught a glimpse of his suitcase, brought from the hotel and similarly violated. He'd been searched. They'd probably tossed the safe house again, too, looking like hell for that wedge.

At least his boots were still on his feet.

His leg came alive first. Bright starbursts of pain emanated from the muscle of his thigh, but at least he could feel it and move it. Next was his midsection, which felt like he'd fallen into an industrial meat tenderizer. Then his head came back online and dwarfed every other pain. He tried to suppress it, but a groan escaped and floated into the black space in front of him.

"Ah, the prodigal son returns." A hand reached out and whipped the blindfold off Joe's eyes. He blinked at the sudden light, and again as Garfield's ugly mug swam into focus above him. Garfield's left eye was bruised and his nose had a bandage over it. Good. At least he'd managed that.

He was lying on bare steel, hands tied behind his back. Someone placed a freezing gelpack on the side of his head, bringing welcome relief. "Can we let him up now?" asked a voice. Joe recognized it but couldn't place it.

Garfield looked a question at him. "What do you say, Joe? We done? I hate to see you trussed up like this."

It hurt, but he nodded. "I guess," he said, and it came out harsh and dry. Someone powered down the restraints on his hands. A hand slipped under his shoulder to help but Joe shook it off. He levered himself off the deck and onto a long, low bench that stretched the length of the wall, matching a second bench on the other side, about eight feet away. He straightened out his clothes and put the pockets back where they should be. A tube of water landed in his hand and he drank it dry.

"Easy on that," said the voice again. Joe turned. To his right sat Ryza, grey robes and all, with a med kit open at his feet. "My name is Ryza," he said before Joe could react. "I'm a representative of the Peter Foundation and these gentlemen have agreed to give me a ride. Mind if I tend to your wounds?"

Interesting. Joe shrugged. Even that hurt. Ryza rummaged around in the kit and came up with a hypospray which he pressed to Joe's arm. "This will help," he murmured, and Joe felt a cool hiss enter his bloodstream. Instantly the pain backed off and a new energy flooded through his veins. Ryza lifted Joe's bloody hand onto a pad and reached for some quick-heal salve.

He let Ryza do his ministrations and looked around. The passenger bay of the runabout was ten feet across by twenty long, mostly metal with plenty of storage lockers and the bare minimum of padding. An open door at one end gave him a glimpse of the pilot and navigator, along with a fine view through the front screen.

Stars, hanging in the beautiful black of space. Dead center lay the small circle of Poundville, slowly growing larger.

The other end of the room had a closed door. Beyond it,

Joe knew, was the cramped and conduit-filled engine room, source of the endless vibrations. He knew the craft, a Moonlifter troop transport runabout. Unbidden, the memory of the control panel filled his mind. He could feel the stick in one hand, thruster paddle in the other. Feel the clunky, utilitarian spacejet respond to his commands.

"Feels good to be back, doesn't it?" Garfield sat opposite, dabbing his own knuckles with salve, that wolfish grin back on his face.

"It's an honor to meet you, sir." A young woman, wearing the same tactical grey but with quarter-moons on her shoulders, sat to Joe's left. He squinted over at her. She came up to his shoulders and was a neat, professional package, from bootzips to badges. A safetied service laser was holstered on her right hip.

She was looking at Joe, God help him, with stars in her eyes.

"Right side, Corporal," he said.

She flashed over into confusion as Garfield chuckled. "Pardon?"

"When you transport a prisoner, sit on their right side. Keeps your weapon away from their hands."

Her eyes widened. "Oh! Yes, sir." She freed her laser and stowed it under the seat. Not that he would have gone for the laser anyway. One blast from that thing would open up the spacejet like a scalpel.

"Details, details," Garfield chuckled. "Maybe now that she's heard it from one of her idols she'll remember. Captain Drive, meet Corporal Novata."

"Idol?" Joe shook his head. "Must have heard you wrong. I'm nobody's idol."

"Hah! Wrong again, boy. You're a legend. The most anti-rebel sorties flown. The fastest Moon-Mars transit in fleet history. The only pilot in the Interstellar Space Force to survive a four-on-one interplanetary space fight. The list goes on. Or had you forgotten?"

He had. Because every sortie, every dogfight with a Resistance jet, had ended up with other people dead. Lots of them.

"Novata," Garfield continued, "take Captain Drive up to the bridge."

Space was every bit as large and beautiful as the last time he'd seen her. The transport's cockpit had a floor to ceiling view, which gave the uninitiated a severe case of vertigo but which filled Joe with an old longing. This was what had drawn him to the ISF in the first place. A million points of brilliant light dotted the deep black of the universe, laid out in the patterns he remembered so well. No matter where he was in the Solar System, facing any direction, he could never be lost. The stars were his friends and he knew them all. This was home.

"Great to meet you, Captain," said the pilot from the left-hand seat. He glanced up from his controls to give Joe that same starry-eyed gaze, even though the two full moons on his lapels pegged him as a captain, Joe's old rank. "We should be docking in seventeen minutes."

Poundville was larger now. Joe could see details from the holo laid out before him. They were headed for the main settlement, Wheeler's mansion large in the center of a sprawling town. Below the asteroid's equator he saw a second grouping of buildings, and off to the right he glimpsed a blue lake before the transport's flight path took it out of view. Ella, he knew, must be around the back side of the big rock.

"Want to take her for a spin?" The pilot was unbuckling his harness, ready to step away and hand Joe the controls.

"Not yet," came Garfield's order from the rear of the transport. "Sit back down, Belltower."

Joe smiled and patted Belltower on the shoulder. "Thanks for the offer. Another time, maybe."

"I'd love to see what you can do, sir. Hope I get the opportunity."

Joe hmphed. "Just point it and fly, that's all. I'm sure you know more about it than I do."

Belltower laughed, and the co-pilot, a lieutenant with Talbot on his name flash, joined in. "I doubt that very much, Captain. Strap in, please, we're on approach."

The deceleration surge threw him against his restraints as they slowed to re-entry velocity. From his seat back in the main room, Joe got to see the Poundville defences at work. Two hundred miles out an alarm sounded as they passed through the detection shield, and Belltower got busy entering a long string of codes to give them access. At fifty miles and the edge of atmosphere they were joined by two Xray close-combat fighters, fast and deadly, as their escort to the ground. Joe was glad he hadn't tried any kind of direct assault. He would never have made it.

Belltower guided them in for a smooth landing in a massive hangar tacked onto the side of the big mansion. As they were hissing through Poundville's atmosphere Joe turned to Ryza, sitting next to him. "So, what brings you up here?"

"Foundation business," Ryza said. "Standard gravity maintenance, planetary observations, that sort of thing. The ISF is kind enough to let us tag along on flights when we need to go somewhere." He avoided looking at Joe. Obviously they were meant to be strangers. Joe played along and stopped asking questions.

"Let's do this," Garfield ordered as the spacejet clicked into its cradle. "Belltower, head over to Hangar Yankee 3.

The rest of you, standard cordon." He turned to Joe and Ryza. "Mr. Monk, always a pleasure. All right, Joe, let's get you to your appointment. Wheeler Pound doesn't like to be kept waiting."

The hangar let onto a maze of plain, utilitarian corridors, all pale, pink Martian concrete and instant wall with a miserly layer of carpeting. The air was a little thin for Joe's liking – even with a Foundation gravity device there was only so much atmosphere the little planetoid could hold on to – and smelled artificial.

Ryza disappeared down a corridor without a backward glance or a word of farewell, obviously familiar with the place and intent on whatever he was up to. Garfield, Novata and Lieutenant Talbot braced Joe in a guard formation and marched him down a different corridor. They were in for a long walk, apparently.

"What does Pound want with you, anyway?" Garfield muttered as they marched. "Near as I can figure, you've done a hundred percent of nothing for the past three years. Now this. You must have something he wants."

Garfield's poker face slipped. He snuck the tiniest sidewise glance at Joe, looking for any sign that Joe knew about the black wedge. Joe kept his own eyes forward, focused on the corridor as he trudged forward.

"Old Wheeler wants to hear about his kid," he answered, truthfully enough. "Seems like Ella has stopped talking to him. Heaven knows why."

Garfield scowled at Joe, working out if his leg was being pulled. Then he let out a barking laugh. "Yeah. She should be thanking us for keeping her safe. The girl's slipped her moorings, if you ask me."

Gradually the quality of construction improved. The air warmed and began to smell of green, growing things. The carpet changed to a thick weave and complex, flowing design. Occasional artwork appeared on the walls. Eventually they stopped in front of a door made of genuine oak. The shipping alone would be worth a Lowlife's wage for a year.

"We stay here," Garfield announced to Joe. He was showing his teeth again. "You go through the door. Good luck." He slapped a wall plate and the door whooshed open.

Chapter 20

Joe stepped into the most elegant conference room he'd ever seen. Two layers of thick, intricately woven Persian rugs – the real deal, not Sea of Tranquility knockoffs – cushioned his feet. Holographic wall panels showed an expansive mountaintop vista with breathtaking views of snowy peaks in all directions. Unseen atmosphere generators gave the room a crisp snowfall scent and a hint of cool breeze to complete the effect.

A long table, carved from the largest piece of translucent, ruby-colored Martian jade he'd ever seen, occupied the room's center. The end closest to Joe was laden with a small feast – turkey, roasted vegetables, fancy desserts, salads, and three bottles of wine. The room was illuminated by a soft, warm light source he couldn't find, as if the molecules of air themselves were lit from within.

Joe got the overall sense of being on a sultan's flying carpet high over a mountain paradise.

"Mr. Drive, Joe, thank you for coming." Wheeler Pound stood on the opposite side of the table, tall and slim and sharp as a mountain ridge. The man was less impressive in person. Until he looked at you. Those piercing blue eyes scanned him from under a receding wave of thick, black hair. His brows drew together as he spotted Joe's damaged appearance. "I told my men not to harm you, that you'd agreed to come peacefully."

Joe held his ground three steps away from the feast as his stomach growled in quiet rebellion. "We had some things to work out."

Wheeler considered, and a thin smile softened the lines of his face. "Ah, history. Blinken was your commanding officer, wasn't he? I should have seen that. You've had a long night, Joe, and a troubled voyage. You must be famished. Help yourself." Pound indicated the spread on the table. He pinched a petit-four and poured a small glass of wine for himself, giving Joe a look over the rim of the glass as he sipped. As if to say, see, it's not poisoned.

Joe knew the food wasn't poisoned. Wheeler's concern for Ella was genuine and he wanted Joe's help. He wasn't about to fly Joe up here just to kill him with gourmet catering.

He grabbed a plate and dug in. Another soldier's maxim: never pass up a meal. Over a slab of turkey he scanned his host in turn. Tall, matching Joe's six-foot-three. Slim build, but his movements betrayed a good level of fitness and coordination. Probably a squash and Zero-Gball player, Joe figured. Maybe does laps in the family lake. He knew Wheeler's age from his research – 73 – but the man before him didn't look a day over 55. A pocketbook that large could buy a few extra years, it seemed.

Wheeler was still smiling, but underneath it was the sadness Joe had noted before. Both the momentary humor and the deeper worry were genuine, he decided. They were at odds with the megalomaniac ruler shown by his research. The man who ran the Solar System with cruelty and force, and who apparently directed the Interstellar Space Force's push against the rebels.

The man who would kill the Moon. Who had imprisoned his only daughter for trying to stop him.

"I'm here, Mr. Pound," he said, washing down a mouthful of pickled Venusian ghostberry flan with a swig of fine merlot. "What would you like to talk about?"

That sadness edged closer to the surface. Despite himself, Joe felt an ember of sympathy for Wheeler kindle in his mind. "My daughter, of course," Wheeler said. "You don't have any children, do you, Joe? No, that's not the soldier's way, is it. A strange thing happens when a man becomes a father. He starts to care."

Wheeler put the wine glass down, his thirst forgotten. "Ella and I were close, Joe. We fished together, did you know that? I had silver wingfish brought up from the lakes of Antarctica and put in Pound Pond, just so I could watch her catch them. We had conversations that lasted hours, silly ones and deeper ones, too. We laughed together in those days. Ella touched my heart, Joe. More than you could ever know."

"And then she grew up and saw you," Joe said. Careful with your words, he chided himself, you want to get out of this alive. But there was only so much sentimentality he could take.

Wheeler considered the rebuke and decided not to trigger whatever dreadful lasers were hidden in the woodwork. Joe could practically see the decision in the man's eyes. "She grew up, yes," he said, "but she did not see me. She saw what the blazing fire of youth showed her, Joe, that burst of awareness that paints everything in primary colors and absolutes. Just like everyone else, she saw my actions but not the vision behind them. And she hardened herself against me."

"So you locked her away."

Pound looked surprised. "For having her own mind? No, I was proud of her new independence, in a way. Our discussions took on a new tone, but we had them. She sought me out to talk with me, try to convince me." He plucked a tiny apple from the spread and held it as he answered. "But then she tired of it. We stopped talking. She refused my contacts. Ella put her opinions into action, without any thought of what she was doing. Without any thought at all. She moved to cripple my plans, Joe. And she's a Pound, so she did it well." He popped the apple into his mouth, savoured one bite and swallowed it down. "That is when I locked her away, as you call it. And that is when she reached out to you."

"And you know why." Joe kept it as neutral as he could. There were objectives to accomplish, and he couldn't do that if he were blown to bits.

Wheeler's expression soured. "A stupid plan, desperate and doomed to fail. I cannot abide desperation. It has fathered some of humanity's largest mistakes."

Joe tried one of the tiny apples. It glistened with sugar and made his taste buds sing. "So ask your questions, Mr. Pound."

"Call me Wheeler, please. What did she say? How is she? Tell me everything." Wheeler's blue eyes drilled through him again, eager for whatever Joe could give.

Sugar might be fine for the apples, but it wouldn't do for Wheeler Pound. Joe gave it to him straight. "She's pissed, Wheeler," he said. "Of course she is, being locked up in an actual goddamned ivory tower. That's no way to treat anybody, let alone family. So she doesn't like your politics. Doesn't like the way you use the Interstellar Space Force like a private, hired army to protect your profits and smash the little people into obedience. She's not alone in that, I can tell you. Suck it up, Wheeler. You either listen to her, because she's right, or you agree to disagree. Don't force her into making terrible choices, sir. Because she will. She has your stubbornness." He took another apple. "Give it a rest, Pound. Let Ella go."

Wheeler Pound looked like he'd just been slapped. Joe enjoyed the apple, wondered if he would ever get to taste another, and held his breath.

Then Pound burst into a single, explosive laugh. "Hah! Do you know how many years it's been since I've been scolded? You remind me of Ella, Joe. Your honesty is commendable, and worth the price of bringing you up here. But your naiveté is not. Like Ella, you do not see the big picture. And like her, you would not understand if I tried to tell you, so I won't bother. I also will not be letting her go. In her current frame of mind she is still a danger to herself, and to others. Thank you for making that clear to me."

Joe breathed again and set down his wine glass. He'd survived the encounter, which had been objective number one. Now for objective two. "Happy to help. If there's nothing more, you said something about a trip back home."

"Ah, yes. Just one more thing." A touch of embarrassment touched Pound's eyes. "This does not come easily to me. But I feel I must apologize for sending the assassin. It was – rash."

Impressive, Joe thought. The expression looked real. But Wheeler Pound was constitutionally incapable of either embarrassment or apology. Now it was Joe's turn to act. He hoped he could be as convincing.

"Assassin? What assassin? You mean that first squad tonight? That was just business. I don't take it personally."

Pound's blue eyes examined him again. Looking for the slightest clue that Joe knew anything about the man in the wrinkle-free suit. About why Wheeler hadn't heard from him, or heard about the success of whatever that assassin was supposed to do to the Moon. Looking to see if Joe knew anything at all about a little, black wedge. The force of that gaze was a physical thing, and Joe had to resist the urge to lean away from it.

Pound blinked. "That's good, then. As we discussed, Joe, a private spacejet is waiting to take you back to Heaviside." He twiddled two fingers in the air and the wallet in Joe's pocket buzzed. "That will compensate you for your time. If my daughter tries to contact you again, you will do the responsible thing and refuse. Have a nice life on the Moon, Joe Drive. I do not expect I will see you, or hear about you, again."

The door whished open. Corporal Novata stood at rigid attention on the other side, now sporting a thick-barrelled stunner at her hip and a Surebeam 450 autorifle on her shoulder. Joe grabbed a couple of oranges off the table, tossed one to a surprised Novata, and followed his guard into the hall.

Chapter 21

Joe and Novata stomped down the corridor towards the hangars. He smelled a burst of bright, sweet citrus in the corridor's still air and heard the corporal busily slurp through her orange as she walked behind him. He understood. Soldiers didn't get Earthside treats like that, and she didn't want the others seeing it. It was a marvel that any ISF grunt ever believed the 'soldiers are Elites' lie. But then again, he had.

Garfield and Lieutenant Talbot waited around a corner. Joe thought about his failure to secure Ella's release and allowed disappointment to take over his features. "Don't start," he grumbled as Garfield fell into step beside him.

"Aww," Garfield said, peering into Joe's face with a delighted grin. "You look like a kid who didn't get his way. What, did you demand he let his daughter go? You did, didn't you! Hah! I admire your stones, Captain Drive, but you lost again. Must be a familiar feeling by now."

He laughed as Joe's expression sunk into irritation, then dropped the derision. "Seriously, Joe, what did you expect? That you'd lay it out for the leader of the Solar System and he'd suddenly see the error of his ways? If you thought that, you weren't paying attention." His voice hardened into a parade ground order. "What's the first rule of situational awareness?"

"See what's there. Everything that's there. Nothing that isn't." Belltower, Novata and Lieutenant Talbot reeled off the answer in unison. To his disgust, Joe felt his lips mouthing the words along with them.

"Right. And the potential for a change of heart wasn't there, Captain. I didn't even have to be in the room to know that. Wheeler Pound doesn't have a heart. Even if he did, do you think you'd be the one to change it?" He poked Joe in the ribs, a gentle finger jab. "I'm really sorry, Joe, but you don't have it in you. Not anymore."

Joe lifted his head out of his own thoughts and looked at Garfield, actually surprised at the regret he heard in the old soldier's words.

"You know what he's doing, right? Aside from holding his daughter captive?"

"Sure." Garfield stayed shoulder to shoulder with Joe as they marched. "He's keeping the Solar System from chaos, that's what. Humanity has it good now, Joe. The Elites run the place, the Lowlifes do the work, and everybody gets by. Those rebels you're so fond of? They want to tear it all down, with no thought for what that means. Imagine what it would look like. No order? No government? That's chaos, and Wheeler Pound prevents it. The ISF prevents it."

"Through bombs and death." Joe's voice rose, echoing off the corridor. He stopped, forcing all of them to stand still. "Like what you had me do. Entire villages gone, Blinken. Bodies everywhere. I saw it. I didn't program it, but I dropped the bombs. I saw what they did. That's what your precious order looks like." Now he was shouting.

Garfield nodded. "Yes, it does. And you know what? It's

working. The rebels are almost done. We've got a few big knockout blows planned for them, and it will be over. But it wasn't like that a few months ago." He laughed again. "That girl of yours? She gave us a good run. Stole her daddy's funds, stole his supplies, and for awhile the Resistance had us. They were winning. As soon as Pound locked her up – that was my idea, by the way – we got the upper hand back. Now it's almost over."

Garfield moved forward again. Belltower gave Joe a gentle nudge and they all resumed walking. Joe clenched a fist around the orange he still carried. "I don't pay much attention to politics. Maybe not as much as I should have." He thought about Dora, her current flame Ray, the others he knew in The Shaft. All just getting by. Never getting ahead, getting better. Never having the chance. "But I do know that the order you're speaking of stinks. Do the rebels want chaos? I don't know, I never asked them. Never cared. But maybe," he returned Garfield's finger jab, "they want what's on the other side of chaos. Whatever that looks like, it'll be better than what they have now."

"Pah." Garfield dismissed it with a spat breath. "We're almost at the finish line in this war, Captain. You know, I'd really love to have you back. Finish what we started together. I've built some crack teams for the ISF," he looked back over his shoulder, "but you're the best soldier I've ever trained. I want you back, son." He faced forward again. "But only if you're up to muster. And so far, I don't see it."

They walked a few minutes in silence, turning down plain, unadorned hallways Joe didn't remember. They were taking him to a different hangar than before. Made sense. The little Moonlifter transport they'd arrived in couldn't do a Mars to Moon run.

Garfield's words stung. Joe had spent three years tucked

away from the world. Not involved. Had it made him soft? Had it cost him something? All he'd wanted was a bit of breathing room to reorient his life. He followed along two steps behind Garfield, feeling the wash of his commander's disappointment.

They approached a Y-split in the corridor, identical to half a dozen they'd already passed. Belltower made to steer them down the left branch when Garfield's voice stopped him.

"You know what? Change of plans." Garfield turned around and the expression on his face was bright and crystal-hard. "I hate to see you like this, Joe, you're sad as a wet rag. So I'm going to complete your mission for you. Belltower, carry on as instructed. Take Joe here to Heaviside and let him get back to his sorry excuse for a life. I'm staying on Poundville for a little bit longer." He broke into a huge, child-eating grin. "I'm going to fly down to the South Mansion and take out Ella Pound. It's what she paid you for, after all." With that, Garfield spun on his heel and took off down the right-hand corridor.

"Wait!" Joe lunged after him, but Belltower, Novata and Lieutenant Talbot held him back. "She doesn't want that! She only thinks she does! I was never – " But Garfield was gone. He struggled some more, but they had a firm lock on him.

"This way, sir," Belltower grunted as they pushed Joe down the other hall. "Don't make us." Novata had taken up station five feet behind, the Surebeam autorifle strapped down to make way for the stunner in her hand. Joe was going to the Moon whether he wanted to or not.

And Ella was going to get her wish.

Chapter 22

He struggled, tested their holds, but both men were battle-strong and trained. His blood raced, pounding through his skull. Then he forced himself to calm down. Any serious attempt at a break for Garfield would only mean he went to the Moon feet-first. With an effort he stopped the inner scream building in his mind and let them walk him forward.

The air grew thin and sharp with the tang of old ozone. They were close to the hangar. A side door opened ahead of them and a grey-hooded figure emerged into the corridor. Ryza stood still while they approached.

"Mind if I join you?" he asked. "I hear you're headed Luna way."

The request was a formality. Peter Foundation representatives got rides from the ISF wherever they needed to go. The tradition was so ingrained Joe had never seen a request refused. Belltower shrugged, and Ryza fell in beside Joe.

"Pleasure to see you again, traveler," he murmured. "I trust your adventure was successful?"

"Not especially," Joe mumbled back. He didn't feel much like talking.

"Well then, I trust your adventure is not yet over."

Joe spared him a glance, and Ryza's clear, blue eyes burned with the question. What have you got left in you, Captain? The truth was, he didn't know. He offered no answer.

Ryza kept quiet for a moment. "These are important days we're in, aren't they?" he asked the group as they walked.

"Yes sir, Mr. Monk," replied Belltower, his voice tinged with excitement. "The Commander says we're almost done with the rebels. A few more tricks up our sleeve and that will be it." He tossed a look back at Ryza's grey hood. "He doesn't give us much detail, though. Would you know anything about it?"

Always gather intel. Garfield's old advice rang in Joe's mind and he admired Belltower's tactic. Ryza chuckled. "Not too much, I'm afraid. I know the situation carries a lot of gravity, enough to move worlds. There are just a few missing pieces to be put into place and it will all be over. I do know," and here he glanced at Joe again, "that something is afoot, even as we speak."

The three soldiers laughed. Typical vague Foundation-speak, heavy on the rhetoric and light on anything useful. Joe didn't laugh. He thought, hard and fast.

They turned the last corner and Belltower punched in the code to roll open a massive pressure door at the corridor's end. A blast of cool air, rich with the smells of machinery and ozone, washed over them. They stepped into the hangar.

Joe sucked in a breath of air through his teeth as his insides gave a peculiar lurch. A Celestial Arrow rested in the dock, sleek and silver, her perfect lines marred only by the Pound Enterprises logo on the main hatch. A fast, unarmed ISF reconnaissance ship, at home in deep atmosphere, high orbit or interplanetary space, the Arrow could lift out of an Earth-sized gravity well in under four minutes. Its Halliwell ion drive was tuned for maximum performance and could power the Arrow anywhere in the Solar System in half the time of a commercial transport. The Pounds had retooled it as a comfortable, custom-built racing yacht.

The Celestial Arrow was his favourite ride. He knew the controls better than he knew his console back in Heaviside.

They escorted him through the hatch and into a sumptuous interior vastly different than any Arrow he'd ever seen. Smooth, padded walls, Persian carpets again, first class seats, more of that everywhere-at-once lighting. Nice retrofit. He took a seat next to the pilot's bulkhead and rolled the orange between his palms as Belltower moved forward to take the controls. Ryza saw Joe's positioning and a tiny gleam flashed through the young monk-engineer's eyes.

Joe yawned and stretched into the comfort of his chair, weary after his long struggles. He regarded the orange. It practically glowed, it was so perfectly ripe. He scratched the skin and gave it an appreciative sniff.

He could see Belltower's shoulder through the bulkhead door. Novata and Lieutenant Talbot grabbed seats a little out of arm's reach on opposite sides of the cabin, a standard triangulation guard. As Belltower went through his preflight checklists, Novata and Lieutenant Talbot saw Joe's yawn and relaxed, just a little. Novata dropped the stunner to her lap.

Belltower leaned his head back through the bulkhead door. "Destination's Luna, right?"

"Yeah, around the back. Heaviside spaceport. Home sweet home." He yawned again, huge and obvious. Lieutenant Talbot and Novata relaxed some more. Novata found herself copying his yawn and stopped it.

The Arrow left its dock with the smallest click and they were airborne. Belltower was a decent pilot. Joe watched as they backed out of the hangar. Then they were in the air over

Wheeler's Northwest mansion, pivoting for a breakaway burn in the bright light of day.

"Mind if I watch?" Joe reached for the center buckle of his harness and tapped it with the orange in his hand, releasing the complex webbing that held him to his seat.

"Hey now," said Novata as Joe rose, but that was as far as she got. He winged the orange at her as hard as he could in the cramped quarters. It caught her square on the forehead, spraying juice in all directions. He snatched the stunner off her lap, aimed and fired.

"Wonk," burped the stunner as a targeted wall of sound caught Novata in the chest and threw her to the back of the cabin. She melted to the floor, out for the duration. The stunner hummed as it began its three-second recharge cycle. Joe pivoted to face Lieutenant Talbot. The kid was on his feet, face determined and arms ready for a takedown.

Joe shouldered the stunner's strap to free his hands, grabbed both of the seats in front of him, hooked his feet under their legs and braced. The Arrow rolled upside down. They were still well within Poundville's gravity field, so Lieutenant Talbot rolled with it. It wasn't a barnstorming, Fall Fair barrel roll, lazy and delightful. This was a snap turn. The Arrow righted and kept on going, rolling again. The soldier tumbled around like a loose marble, banging on ceiling, chairs, floor. Ryza had kept himself strapped in and whooped with delight.

When the Arrow righted itself again, Joe was ready. The stunner was recharged. It said "Wonk," again. Lieutenant Talbot flew up against the rear bulkhead and dropped to the floor next to the freshly-tumbled Novata.

Ryza was laughing, obviously enjoying himself. Joe found some restraints in a side compartment and tossed them to the monk. Ryza set about securing the unconscious soldiers.

Joe dodged into the copilot's seat and levelled the humming stunner at Belltower. "Trained by O'Reilly?" he asked.

Belltower nodded, keeping his hands on the controls. "Yes, sir. In the event of a cabin takeover, roll it."

"Usually works. Worked for me this time."

Belltower threw a shrug towards the cabin. "Are they all right?"

"Nothing broken. They'll be awake in a few minutes."

"So, where to now? Not home, I'm guessing."

"Not quite yet," Joe said. He handed over a set of restraints. "If you please."

Belltower locked the electronic cuffs over his wrists and awkwardly traded places with Joe. "All right if I stay up here?" he asked. "I'd love to watch your work. You come with a hell of a reputation."

Joe levered himself into the pilot's seat and snapped the harness into place. "Yeah, why not."

He was back at the controls of a spacejet. It felt like slipping into an old, time-softened shirt that had molded itself to his body. He caressed the directional sensors and the Arrow responded beautifully, arcing back and forth through the upper atmosphere of the small asteroid. "The South Mansion," he said. "Where Ella is. Where the asshole is going."

Belltower gave the heading and Joe made the course correction. Then, pausing a moment for effect, he eased the thruster forward. The Halliwell drive purred to life and he shot through the manufactured atmosphere of Poundville, a hundred feet above the ground, hurtling towards vengeance.

Chapter 23

Almost immediately the comms squawked into life. "Flight X371 from Northern Control. We show you on a course deviation. Verify and explain."

Joe glanced over at Belltower in the copilot's seat. "Are you going to say the right things?" he asked.

"Yeah, sure," Belltower said, looking glum but resigned. "We're just going to get shot down anyway. Might as well delay it as long as possible."

Joe gestured at the comms and Belltower answered. "Northern Control, this is Flight X371. Sealed orders, came with the detainee. New destination is South Palace detention center."

A pause. Then, "We have no record of new orders."

Belltower said, "Yeah. Like it's the first time that's happened. They want this guy down south, that's all I know."

"Typical. All right, your flight path is updated. Safe travels." The comms clicked off.

"Thanks," Joe said. "No duress codes. Mind if I ask why?"

Belltower still didn't look happy about it. "Like I said,

sir. Your reputation precedes you, and I'd like to see what you can do. But I still don't think we're going to make it. The security around here was built by an expert." He turned to gaze out the viewscreen at the landscape screaming past below them. "And I don't like what they've done, or what the Commander is doing," he added softly. "Ms. Pound's a nice lady. She's a prisoner, and old man Pound has turned us into jail guards. It's not right."

"My thoughts exactly."

Ryza stuck his nose into the cockpit. He'd thrown his hood back to reveal his close-cropped blond fuzz and a face full of excitement. "The other two are secured," he reported. "Want me to do anything with the captain?"

Joe shook his head. "No, I think Belltower here will behave himself. I didn't get the chance to ask before, Ryza. What the hell are you doing here?"

"Wait, you two know each other?" Belltower raised an eyebrow. "Good job, I didn't catch it."

"Thanks," said Ryza, flushed with pride. "What am I doing here? If it's the Foundation asking, I am here to observe and report, influencing human behaviour and the outcome of situations as little as possible." It rolled off his tongue like a company mission statement. Which it probably was. Then the monk's voice changed. "If you're asking, Mr. Drive, I am here to help in whatever way I can. The Algorithm keeps saying that this is a pivotal moment in humanity's evolution, but it's annoyingly sparse on details. The group who interpret the Algorithm through the Prognosticator, the Foundation Council, are old and stuck. All they want to do is have us sit back and watch."

"Which isn't how you fly," Joe said. "An important moment, eh? But no idea how?"

"The Algorithm gives hints. Your name came up. And

Ella Pound's. That little item you're carrying. But after that, the math gets muddy. The Council sent me to keep an eye on you, and nudge you into action, but after that only to watch. I think they're afraid to act."

Joe regarded the young man with a bit more respect. "And you're afraid not to."

Ryza wasn't smiling now. "I've seen some of the equations, Joe. The Council is right about this moment being important. Not just today, but the next year. Everything will change. For better. Or very much for the worse." He shook off the seriousness and raised a hand, palm up. "So I'll do what I can. Speaking of which, I think it might be time for me to take possession."

"It's about time. My hands are busy. Here." He kicked the right shoe off his foot. The one that had lost its heel and been so expertly repaired by the Lowlife shoe lady. Ryza picked it up. "Press the heel's inner edge."

The monk examined the thick, rubberine heel, then tapped the inner side next to the sole. A small drawer popped out. He opened it the rest of the way and got very still.

"Oh my," he murmured. Then he flipped the black wedge out into his hand. He rotated it back and forth. "Such a small thing. So far from home."

He tore his eyes from the wedge and spoke again. His voice had gained some authority. The monk actually sounded deeply angered. "The Council were fools not to have seen this. Thank you, Joe, for safeguarding it, and for stopping that man. You saved the Moon from a very bad day."

Joe checked his instruments, checked them against the stars all around them, and made a minor course correction. "Can you tell what that thing was going to do?"

"That all depends on the device settings. The wedge is like the Halliwell drive on this ship. It provides the force, but you decide how much and where it's directed. A skilled operator can tune a Foundation Device to gravitize a village, a hemisphere, or a planet. Or all three at once to different levels. I don't think we'll ever know what his target was, Joe. He could have flattened a building. Or a city. Or," Ryza hefted the heavy, black wedge, "he could have killed the Moon."

Belltower shuffled in the copilot's seat, getting as far away from the wedge in Ryza's hand as his restraints permitted. Joe pursed his lips and stared straight ahead. "So it's that evil."

Ryza's face was dark. "Afraid so. Doesn't speak well of those who commissioned it. And even worse," he muttered, "for those in my own organization who allowed this to happen. Very few people at the Foundation could have made this wedge."

"What I don't understand," Joe concluded, "is why. Something like that has to serve a purpose. Luna's mines provide some of the most vital metals in the inner planets. The Moon is Earth's staging platform for planetary travel. Why hurt it?"

Belltower and Ryza looked at each other. Ryza spoke. "I guess you've been out of touch, Joe. Everyone knows the Resistance is based on Venus, somewhere outside Aphrodite, right? But in the past year they've made huge inroads on the Moon. It was easy, with all the Lowlife towns and the mines. People are sick of those jobs. Sick of sending everything down the well to Earth, and having to stare at it hanging in the sky every night. The Moon is a hotbed of rebel activity and it's a stone's throw from the Home Alliance. Too close for comfort."

Pieces fell into place. The increasing tension he'd felt around Heaviside. The graffiti, the rebel red fist breaking away from the Earth's blue-green one, popping up everywhere.

"Wheeler was behind this," he said. "The first squad he sent ransacked my stuff to find that." He shrugged at the wedge, which Ryza was tucking into his robes.

"The Commander is his man on the ground," Belltower muttered. "No way he didn't know about this. It's one of those knockout punches he's been talking about to take care of the rebels once and for all. Commander Garfield probably hired the assassin."

The console began a quiet, intrusive beeping. An alarm. Belltower pointed to the viewscreen where a tiny red dot hung suspended in the layer of cloud in front of them. "Proximity alert, friendly," he explained. "We should see it in ..."

Another spacejet emerged from the cloud layer. The Moonlifter transport that had carried them up from Canal City. "Garfield," Joe growled. He waved the middle two fingers of his right hand over the sensors and flicked the Halliwell drive into max-atmosphere high. The Celestial Arrow jumped for the other ship.

"Hey, this bird's unarmed," Belltower warned.

"That's what you think," Joe answered.

Chapter 24

They were five hundred feet off the deck, below them a smooth, rolling expanse of treetops and grass. The Poundville forest. Garfield's ship was slower than the Arrow, less maneuverable, but it had the same alert system. Garfield would know he had company.

And it had weapons. Including ship-mounted stunners, hundreds of times more powerful than the one at Joe's side.

Joe was watching for it. He saw the ripple distort the edges of the transport. "Stunner wave!" he called out and swerved the Arrow to one side. The left wingtip was caught by the powerful sound wave. The Arrow shuddered in midair but flew on, unharmed.

He lifted the spacejet another five hundred feet, dropping all of their stomachs through the floor. "I'll just go buckle in," said Ryza, a little green. His head disappeared back into the main cabin.

"Make sure those other two are strapped down," Joe called after him. After giving the monk a few seconds to get secured he pinched his fingers together over the sensors. The Arrow pivoted on its axis and pointed straight down at the transport below them.

Joe blasted the jets to full. "Whoa!" Belltower shouted, but Joe ignored him. They headed for the ground as fast as the air would let them.

They flew past the nose of Garfield's ship, Belltower meeping in protest. Joe spread his fingers and the Celestial Arrow responded beautifully, arcing into level flight a hundred feet above the forest. Trees waved at them as they passed.

Joe looked up. The transport had been thrown into a crazy spin by the jetwash. It cartwheeled, losing altitude, out of control. As he watched the spacejet did a sweet, complicated looping maneuver and found its controls again. It levelled out. Impressive.

The comms crackled to life.

"Nice trick, Captain Drive!" Garfield's voice was practically ebullient. "Didn't see that one coming. But you've gotten old, son. Soft as Moon-cheese. You're not getting anywhere near the princess. Don't worry, I'll finish your job for you."

The transport was above and behind them. "Watch it!" yelled Belltower as another alarm went on the panel, this one more urgent. It had been years since Joe had heard the sound, but the memory of it was burned into his brain.

Laser lock.

His hands did their thing, as they had years ago. The Arrow bucked as he cut the engines and threw the spacejet into a moment's reverse, then nothing. Stalled in midair, the plane dropped like a stone. The world outside the viewscreens blazed red. A strip of forest below them erupted into bright, crackling fire. The thunderclap of the combat laser beam so close to the cockpit practically deafened him.

He kicked the Arrow into full reverse and regained the flight controls, bringing the craft up behind Garfield. "Got a rear cannon," he heard Belltower say from the end of a ten-mile pipe. Helpful, but unnecessary. He knew the Moonlifter's armaments.

He also knew its limitations. The biggest of which was its pilot, Blinken Garfield.

"Missed me," he said over the comms, his voice as smooth and unruffled as he could make it while dancing furiously over the controls. "You know, Blink, maybe you're not up to this. What say I cut you some slack? Go back and land that tub, and we'll forget that you were ever about to go murder an innocent woman."

The laser lock alarm sounded again. Joe felt Belltower tense in the copilot's seat, but the seasoned soldier didn't yell this time. A flick of his fingers and the Arrow flashed its side maneuvering jets, normally only used in space station docking. The Arrow slid sideways in a move that strained every weld in the fuselage and confused the hell out of the panel's flight indicators, but it held together. The laser bolt fizzed by off the port wing.

"No? All right by me." Joe feathered the controls, aimed the Arrow carefully, and waved the Halliwell drive back to atmospheric maximum. At the same moment a thunk and whir came through the floor from the spacejet's undercarriage.

"Wha'?" Belltower gasped as the acceleration pinned them to their seats. He knew the sound as well as Joe did. Joe had just dropped the landing gear.

The Celestial Arrow shot forward, straight for the transport. Garfield tried a fast fade to landward, copying Joe's earlier move, but Joe was ready and compensated. As they neared a collision Joe fired the maneuvering jets again, dodged the Arrow to the right and down.

An ear-shattering DING rang through the fuselage and the Arrow shuddered, then levelled out. Joe cut the momentum and swung the spacejet around in a lazy arc. There was no rush. He already knew what he'd see.

The transport twirled in crazy circles, headed for the trees. Its right wing hung loose, practically torn off by the Arrow's landing gear. "Might be unarmed," Joe commented, "but she's got a pretty strong foot." He toggled the landing gear back into the belly of the craft.

"There he goes!" Belltower pointed as the transport's cockpit opened up and a streak of rocket exhaust ejected Garfield's chair into the bright day. The transport crashed into the woods below as Garfield's auto-lander set him down in a small meadow.

With a muffled whoomp! the transport burst into flame, taking the nearby trees with it. "We going down there to pick him up?" Belltower asked. He glanced over at the look on Joe's face and didn't ask again.

The comms had crackled into life, Northern Control demanding to know what was up and another unit called Safety One organizing a fire response. Joe ignored them all, reset the coordinates for Ella's prison, and set the Arrow back on course.

Chapter 25

"All right, all right, you live up to your reputation, Captain Drive." Belltower was practically squirming in the copilot's seat, white-faced and almost babbling. "I've never even heard of anything like that. The Commander won't soon forget it. But that was the easy part." He gestured out the viewscreen at the fast-moving countryside below them. "I'm telling you, the security's too tight around the Mansions. You're a great pilot, maybe even the best. But we won't make it."

Joe caught the plea in the statement. His butt was back in a pilot's seat and it felt good. His hands were at home with the controls. A little spot inside his chest was ready to sing, it was so happy. No matter what lay between him and Ella Pound, it would be no match for the nimble Arrow and his skill. Probably. Maybe. He was willing to risk it.

But he was risking more than himself. Belltower, Novata and Lieutenant Talbot were on board. Ryza was somewhere just behind the bulkhead. If he went down, got blown to dust, so did they. Did he have the right to put their lives up against the odds?

The comms channel was relaying a steady stream of

coded messages, tight and fast, the entire Poundville garrison getting updated on the situation. Belltower stared over at him, a bead of sweat rolling down his cheek. He heard a series of muffled exclamations from the two in the back as they tried to add emphasis to Belltower's appeal.

Joe caught sight of the Saturns on Belltower's shoulder and the answer came, cold and clear. Those three were soldiers. They'd taken him hostage, tried to stun him, been his armed escort off the planet. Danger and violence were their job. They would take their chances with him, whether they wanted to or not.

That left one more. He leaned over and stuck his head through the door. "Ryza? What do you think?"

The monk stepped into the doorway. A small but complex-looking device was in his hand, and he was looking at it and grinning. "The Algorithm says we don't die by falling out of the air."

Joe spared a moment to glare over his shoulder. "I thought you said the Algorithm was too complex to understand. That you need the Prognosticator to interpret it. And that the Prognosticator takes up an entire room." A grin touched his face. "And didn't you say the Council are the only ones allowed to look at it?"

Ryza held up the thing in his hand. It looked like a screen caught in a spider's web that had also snagged an entire drawer of kitchen implements. "I'm an engineer."

"Hah! You rebel." Joe paused. "You know what I mean. So if we don't die by falling out of the air, how do we? And when, for hell's sake?"

Ryza shrugged. "No idea. It doesn't work like that. Fifty-fifty we survive the day, that's as close as it gets. But we don't die in this craft. Rockets to full, captain."

Ryza's face was flushed, his eyes lit up with a glow Joe

hadn't seen in years – the glow of a new recruit during their first live-fire exercise. "'Rockets to full?' You are one crazy-ass monk. Strap yourself in." He turned back to Belltower. "Intel, please. What's out there?"

Belltower looked caught in a trap. He jerked his gaze back at his fellow soldiers, then out the viewscreen, then back and forth a couple more times. A soldier didn't reveal his army's positions. But his neck was on the line. Joe gave him a minute to chew on the ethics.

"I can fly in blind," Joe suggested, lifting the Celestial Arrow over a low hill. "Just reduces our chances. A lot. You know, I've seen some action, but I've never been hit by an artillery stunner. Tell me, does the sonic wave rip your arms off, or do you just turn to goo?"

"It's not stunners," Belltower finally spoke. "It's autocannons. A ring of them, every five hundred feet. They shoot a hundred bolts a minute with pinpoint targeting. Autocannons can roast a bird to perfection in midair, or turn a spacejet into orbital shrapnel." Muted howls of protest came from the two in the back, but mainly for show, the noises didn't last long. "Then the garrison itself. No grunts on that crew, they know what they're doing. And if you get through them," his voice got quiet, "then there's the lifebot."

Joe questioned the captain about specifics and placements, then settled in for the flight. The comms kept humming coded commands. "Most of that's fire control in the forest," Belltower offered, "but some of it is for you. They're mobilizing a detachment and waking up the mansion garrison. Three spacejets, twenty-four soldiers. They'll be here in about 20 minutes."

"Plenty of time." He and the Arrow ate up the miles, low and fast over waving grassland that had replaced the forest below them. Way ahead Joe could make out farmed fields and pastures. They were past the equator now, the red marble of Mars hanging above them in the sky, and only a few minutes from the South Mansion.

The first line of defences should be around here somewhere ... He saw it. A line of low hills perforating the grasslands, natural enough except for their military regularity. A thousand feet between each hill.

The same moment he saw them, they saw him. The two hills directly in front lost their tops. Earth and grass sprayed in all directions as a wicked-looking set of barrels surged out of the ground, gimbal-mounted and topped by seeker dishes. They lifted from rest position, spun around and locked on.

Joe reacted. Already low to the landscape, he punched it lower. He kept the landing gear up, but heard the hiss as long grasses brushed the belly of the jet. He edged the Halliwell drive as fast as his reflexes dared and focused on the dips and curves of the land in front of the ship.

Autocannons were precise and deadly. The air shattered as a rapidfire series of high-energy bolts seared past directly overhead. He felt the cabin heat up with their passage and tucked the jet even lower. The weapons were designed to rotate and fire in any direction from straight vertical to almost horizontal. With one safeguard. They couldn't fire completely flat, along the ground. The bolts traveled for miles, and melting towns was considered bad optics.

Another volley passed overhead as Joe kept the spacejet in the gullys, aiming for the low space between the two cannons. He flew around the side of a low rise and there it was, an expanse of smooth ground between the two black guns. They spun furiously on their mounts, trying to get a fix on him.

He screamed through the gap just as somebody, somewhere, realized his tactic and removed the cannons' safeties. Both barrels dipped, levelled, and fired. He goosed the Halliwell drive to Mach 1 as both gun emplacements erupted in dirt and flame from each other's fire.

The Arrow bucked from the shock wave, its nose kissing earth. He eased back to normal cruise speed – Mach 1 at ground level was too insane even for him – and called out, "Everybody okay?"

He'd been too focused on flying to hear the screams. Now Belltower, Novata and Lieutenant Talbot quieted down. Ryza let out another delighted hoot and began laughing.

"You two are crazy as Neptune rounders!" Belltower said when he caught his breath. "I've never seen flying like that in my life!"

"The paint on the rear bulkhead's blistered," called Novata, more in control than her captain, "and the mechanics don't sound right. That last blast was pretty close."

The Arrow handled fine, but felt a little shaky in the controls. "Ryza, go check it out. Okay, Belltower, what's next?"

Belltower composed himself. "The garrison. You've got my respect, Captain Drive, but I gotta say, these guys are next-level. They aren't ISF soldiers. They're a specialist unit. Air force."

That didn't sound right. "So what kind of machines do they fly?"

Belltower shook his head. "No, Drive. They don't fly spacejets. They just fly."

The grassland had given way to manicured lawns. Up ahead Joe saw a massive stone wall, maybe ten feet high, circling a huge estate. The South Mansion, he presumed. Tucked up against the inside of the wall were several military barracks and sheds next to a small landing pad. He spotted the glint of sunlight off windows from a building on the horizon before his attention was drawn back to the barracks.

A swarm of soldiers ran for the landing pad, weighed down with large, heavy packs.

"Here they come," muttered Belltower.

"You really need to work on your attitude," Joe said. The soldiers formed a ring around the edge of the landing pad, then lifted off the ground. Fast, in tight formation, swinging in the Arrow's direction and widening their circle into an enveloping net.

"Whoa!" He'd never seen the like. The Arrow shot skyward at his command, running away from the flying soldiers as he tried to figure them out. "Armaments?" he called to Belltower.

"Nobody knows," Belltower replied. "They keep to themselves, and nobody who has gone against them ever survives to tell."

"Great," Joe muttered. And the Arrow had no weaponry at all, not even a wing-mounted stunner. He burned a path through the Poundville atmosphere, straight up. Let's see what their operational ceiling is, he thought.

The ring of airborne soldiers appeared in the viewscreen. They were a mile up now, in thin air and still going strong. Faster than the Arrow. They were close enough that Joe saw full pressure suits. So much for a ceiling. Those rigs could go orbital.

"Captain Joe Drive!" The comms crackled. "You will land your craft at once." No threat, no alternative, just the command. How rude, Joe thought. He jigged his hand in a vicious slash over the flight sensors. The Arrow complained as it slewed to one side. The starboard wingtip headed for the ring of aeronauts like a giant blade.

The airborne soldiers flitted away in a blur. Damn, they're fast as starflies, Joe thought. As quickly as the formation had disbanded it reformed. Joe broke the climb and levelled out, two miles above the surface and racking his brain for more tricks.

The soldiers in his viewscreen grew bumps on their shoulders. The bumps, large disks, detached and flew on their own. Just peachy.

"Repulsor drones!" Belltower exclaimed from the other seat. "I've only heard about those!"

The soldiers hung back as the drones formed a fast-moving net around the nose of the Arrow. Joe felt more than heard a low, strong hum. Then the Arrow stopped listening to him. It slowed. The stall alarm went off. Then the spacejet stopped in midair and hung there. The Halliwell drive's safeties cut in and the engines slowed to idle.

"Captain Drive! You will be taken to ground, where you will surrender and free your captives." Not even a please. Furious at being caught but helpless to do anything about it, Joe took his hands off the controls. The Arrow began to descend towards the ground, held by the repulsor drones that now blanketed the front of the craft.

Deep in his pocket, his link buzzed. He dug it out. 'Working on it,' said a message from an unknown number. 'Ready in five.'

He had a pretty good idea who had sent the message. He placed his hands back on the controls and counted down from five. When he reached zero, nothing happened. "Minus one. Minus two," he began counting out loud. Belltower glanced over, confused, but Joe kept his eyes on the viewscreen.

On minus three the drones fell off the front of the Arrow. The Arrow itself, deprived of thrust and lift, fell along with them. And the air defence unit, suddenly strapped to non-functioning lift packs, fell along with everything else.

His link buzzed again. 'That's it, they've locked me out,' Kate's message said. 'Happy hunting.'

Flaming pulsejets. Joe stared out the viewscreen at the tiny figures, flailing arms and legs as they tumbled through the thin air. At two miles up, they'd fall for an entire minute. Never, ever get on Kate's bad side, he reminded himself. With a jab and a twist of his big hands, he revved the Arrow's engines up and regained control, flying out of the cloud of falling soldiers.

"How the hell did you do that?" Belltower demanded, "I didn't see you twitch or anything." He looked out the viewscreen at the soldiers and their useless flight packs. "Hell's bells. That's gonna hurt. I can't watch."

Joe said nothing. He flipped the Arrow in an aggressive move that brought exclamations from the back cabin and dove for the large, whitewashed building that was now clearly visible across a huge expanse of green lawn. A minute later he dropped the landing gear and set down at the foot of a massive stone staircase that led to the South Mansion's front door.

Ella Pound stood on the top stair in front of the open door. She looked miserable, defiant and startlingly beautiful. Beside her, arms crossed over a bountiful chest, was an amply-proportioned woman in a flower print dress and a stern, glittering ferroplastic mask for a face.

"Oh hells," mumbled Belltower. "It's the lifebot."

Chapter 26

Joe locked out the controls of the Arrow and turned to Belltower. "Coming or staying?" he asked.

"Oh, I'm fine right here, man." Belltower gazed out the viewscreen at the couple on the stairs. "It's your funeral." The comms crackled with more code, and he translated. "They know you've landed. The whole Poundville contingent is up in arms about what you did to the South Mansion garrison. Every spacejet in the lower hemisphere will be here in five minutes."

Ryza poked his head into the cockpit. "These two are secure. What about him?"

Joe got up and headed into the main cabin. He reached back and slapped the cockpit's door panel, then locked it out, too. "He's fine. Let's get this done. The clock is ticking."

They stepped out of the Arrow and across the bit of grass in front of the steps. It had been a long time since Joe had walked on actual, soft Earth grass. He smelled the perfume of fresh lawn as his boots bruised the blades.

Ella gave a small wave. She was back in house-arrest casual, wearing a loose blouse and denim. She looked miserable all over again. Defeated. "Hello Joe. You shouldn't have bothered. It's no use. You were right. My death won't solve anything."

He waved back. "Hey Ella. Yeah, you're right about that. I'm glad you see it. You can still help the Resistance, though, plenty. But not while you're cooped up in this place. Let's get you out of – "

He placed one foot on the first step and the matronly lifebot uncrossed her arms. "You stop right there, young man!" she said. The makers had given her a grandmother's voice. The grandmother you didn't want to visit, the one who never made cookies and kept a rod in the corner of the kitchen. The mass of grey curls on the bot's head quivered with outrage. "This child is under my protection and I won't have the likes of you getting any closer."

"The likes of ... listen, lady, I need to talk to Ella. So if you'll," and that was as far as he got. He planted his foot, headed for the second step, and the lifebot was down the stairs and in his face. The wind from her lightning descent practically blew him backwards. He teetered, balancing on one foot, as the ferroplastic face leaned in.

"Ruffian! Hooligan. Rake. I will not suffer your presence." She said it quietly, breathed it into him, in a tone that dredged up an ancient fear of being caught with his hand in the cookie jar.

A soft hum began to build in the air between them. He felt her bosom start to vibrate. Twin stunners, charging to a massive, flesh-rending burst. There wasn't even time to run.

"Wonderful Mother, magnificent Caretaker," Ryza purred from beside Joe. "Your dedication is astounding, your vigilance is endless." Apparently swayed by the flattery, the lifebot spared him a glance. "But look at this poor excuse of a man in front of you." Ryza swept an arm down Joe's length, like a politician waving off a question. "He is old. Slow. Unarmed. No challenge for you, and no danger to your ward. He has told me himself that he will not harm Ms. Pound. I believe him."

The hum lessened, the static charge in the air dissipated. The lifebot took a step back and turned to Ryza. "You are a monk," she said at last. "A man of peace and gravity. There is no deceit in your eyes." She pivoted back to Joe and the hum picked up again, her voice rising a notch. "Is what he says true? Will you harm my child?"

Joe bit back his usual flippancy and stared into the robot's eyes. "I will not harm Ella Pound. In fact, I've been talking her out of the whole idea."

The lifebot considered this for a long moment. Ella had descended the stairs and now stood behind her. "It doesn't matter, Joe," she said, her voice as empty as her face. "We both know my death would be useless anyway, even if you agreed to it. Which you never did. I'm stuck here. You're not. Go. Please. While you still can."

"Three minutes till company arrives," Ryza murmured beside him.

"Come with us, Ella," Joe said. "You can't do anything from here, true enough. But there's a ton of good you can do out there." He gestured at the sky and all that lay beyond it.

"I have nothing more to give, Joe," she said. "The Endowment is broke. I have no more access to my father's storehouses and weapons caches. I have nothing to help the rebels with. They're losing, Joe. We've all lost."

"You still have yourself." Joe said it with conviction and volume, trying to counter the hopeless whisper in Ella's words. "Look at you, Ella. You're the most recognized face in the Solar System. That's what you can give to the Resistance, a face. A voice. Get out there and tell people what's going on. Do some more fundraising, but this time let people know what they're supporting. You're good at that, right? Maybe even great?"

A glimmer of hope tried to get through the gloom on Ella's face. He fanned it some more, a small part of him wondering where the words were coming from. If he even believed them.

"That's what you have, Ella. That's what your father can never take away from you, and that's why he's locked you up here. He's scared of you. He knows what you can do, and he's frightened to death that you might realize it. Come on, Ella. Let me get you out of here."

"Take my child?" The lifebot's voice got strident. "Over my dead body, young man, and trust me, you're not up to it. I believe you, that you mean no harm to this girl, but you will not take her away from here. This is our home. This is where we belong. This is where we are safe." Those last three declarations were said with the force of basic programming. Unbreakable. Not to be denied.

Joe could practically feel the air behind him compress with the approaching threat. When the spacejets got here they wouldn't be in a talkative mood. He fought against an urge to cut out of this ridiculous situation, save his skin and run back to the Arrow. The gleam of hope was there in Ella's eyes, but still only a hint, struggling to get through. He bristled against the stubborn slump of defeat in her shoulders and gave it one last try.

"Listen, um, Mother," he said, taking a cue from Ryza. "Ella. You're needed, more than you know. The rebels could do with some inspiration right about now." He thought about it, then added, "Did you know your father plans to kill the Moon?"

That shook her. A spot of color bloomed on her cheeks.

"What did you say?"

"Show her, Ryza." The monk took the black wedge out of his pocket and held it up to the light. "Your father had this made. It's designed to spike the Moon's gravity, we're talking huge. Focus it on any spot you like and it would flatten everything. He's the dangerous one here."

Ella had recoiled in shock at the sight of the wedge, obviously familiar with what it was. Now she leaned for it. Ryza made to hand it to her.

The lifebot's arm flashed between them. "No you don't," she said, and snatched the wedge. She examined it thoroughly as the seconds clicked by in Joe's mind, then muttered, "No threat." And handed it to Ella.

"So small," Ella whispered. She flipped it around, caught the laser etching and blanched when she read the truth of Joe's words. She turned back to Ryza, the silent question huge in her eyes. Ryza saw, and answered with a nod.

Ella Pound transformed. Her shoulders straightened. Every vestige of despair left her body and her face. Joe saw the light return to her eyes, hard and bright. He saw the woman from the holos, the one who could sway hearts and convince minds.

She levelled her gaze at him, her decision made. "My father is a monster, Joe. You're right. There's still some good to be done." She stepped down to join Joe and Ryza.

The lifebot barred her passage. "This is our home. This is where we belong. This is where you are safe, my child. Back up the steps and inside, now, there's a good girl." She pushed Ella backwards.

"Mother, you are failing in your duty." Ryza lifted up another step, level with the lifebot. He kept his hands out wide in the ancient gesture of peace, but his voice had grown hard. His words, and their tone, stopped the iron grandmother.

"I never fail, monk. I serve, I protect. I will make my child safe." She paused, then asked, "How do I fail?"

"You are wise, Mother, and you see much, but maybe not all. Access the Poundville network. See what is coming this way."

The lifebot stood listening, head cocked, then pivoted on her heel to look east. "Men. Jets. Weapons. They are coming here."

"Yes," said Ryza, back to purring. "Jets filled with men. Weapons wielded by men. They are angry. They have lost friends and they are angry. Tell me, Mother. What do you think they will do?"

The sparky, grey-haired grandmother stared at Ryza, then at Ella. "Men. Unreliable, angry men. They will destroy. Shoot first and ask questions later, that's them. They will kill you, monk. Destroy your ship. Destroy this house. Shoot at everything, everywhere, till nothing is left."

"That's right, Mother. And the South Mansion is not shielded, is it? Not from that. You know the guns that are coming. They're almost here." Ryza took a step closer to the lifebot, reached out, placed a hand on her shoulder. Either brave or foolish, Joe thought, but the boy was giving it his best. "Ella is safest with us. Joe Drive is the best pilot in the Solar System. He will not let them harm her. But harm is coming, Mother. We have to leave."

Joe saw the lifebot's simple certainty devolve into indecision and confusion. It almost hurt to watch. Ella gently spun the bot around and faced her.

"Thank you, lifebot. Mother. You've kept me safe here. Now I have to leave, and you know that. Danger is coming and Joe here will save me from it." She smiled. "But you can still save me from harm, too, can't you? Even after you let me go? You can still succeed in your duty."

The lifebot slipped from confusion into her new reality. "Yes, child," she said, "you and the monk are right." She jabbed out an arm and grabbed a handful of Joe's shirt. She pulled him close with an awful strength, stared into his eyes. "You are still conflicted, man. Not completely trustworthy. But I believe you will keep my child safe." Pulled him even closer, chest to chest. "You will not fail."

He swallowed. "No, ma'am. I will keep her safe."

She dropped him, spun around and marched down the steps to the grass. "Go, child. You have been unhappy here, I know. Be safe, and be happy." She stuck her feet to the ground in a wide-legged stance and lifted her gaze east. "Leave now, all of you. I will do my job."

***

As the Celestial Arrow rose off the ground, Mother Lifebot 33KY7 amplified her vision to maximum and saw the sky in the east darken with a cloud of spacejets. A laser bolt, fired from far out of range at the airborne Arrow, streaked across the sky until it fizzled out short of the mansion grounds.

She threw her arms wide and thrust her chest to the advancing cloud. "You will not harm my child!" she yelled, feeling the hum within her reaching a crescendo. The front of her flower print dress exploded as the twin stunners fired. The air before her rippled with energy. Seven spacejets in the front of the pack shuddered and disintegrated, catching an eighth with their debris.

Mother Lifebot 33KY7 drained her energy cells for a second fast charge, but the next spacejet was faster. Over the communications net she heard Commander Blinken Garfield say, "I've got the bitch." A laser bolt from the east blew her out of her shoes.

Chapter 27

The cockpit of the Arrow was full to bursting. "Give me some space here," Joe grumbled as he elbowed Ryza out of the way so he could switch off the cabin cooler. That would give them another ounce or two of speed. And right now, speed was the only weapon he had.

"Gotta go orbital, Captain," Belltower pattered from the copilot's seat, clearly nervous again. He had every right to be. The aft screen showed an entire ISF squadron behind them like a swarm of angry hornets. The lifebot, bless her artificial soul, had taken out eight, but at least fifteen more birds chased them across the Poundville sky.

"No! They'll hunt us across the entire Solar System. Head south," Ella insisted. She had squeezed in behind Joe's seat, distractingly close. A subtle scent wrapped around his head, more reminiscent of a summer meadow than the interior of a spacejet.

She frowned a look at Ryza, who hovered in the doorway. Ryza, as surprised as everyone else at the gazillionaire heiress giving tactical advice, gave her a puzzled expression and then seemed to understand something. He chimed in. "Yes, she's right! Head due south. It's our only chance."

Any idea was better than none at all. Joe swung the craft south and gave it all the Arrow could do in atmosphere. The air hissed against the fuselage and the cockpit warmed from the friction. "Okay, south. Why?"

Ryza held up the black wedge. "This is why."

Joe took his eyes off the controls and spun around. The monk was grinning like a fiend, the damn greenhorn. "You have got to be fucking kidding me."

Ryza actually laughed, a tinny edge to it. "Nope. But step on it, I'll need a couple of moments once we get there."

"Step on it, he says," Joe grumbled. "Like I'm doing anything else."

The Arrow screamed through the sky. Night was falling. Mars hung like a red Zero-Gball above and behind them, giving the landscape a reddish tinge as the distant sun set in the west. The comms, which had been crackling with coded communications nonstop since they lifted off, now cleared. Then a single voice broke through into the cockpit.

"Captain Drive! I must say, you put on a good show. But you appear to be outnumbered, son. Set 'er down. We'll have a beer in the officer's mess and discuss your future in the ISF."

Joe slapped the comms unit. "Garfield, how many times do I have to shoot you out of the sky? Quit talking, old man, because I don't believe a single word you say."

The cockpit filled with a slow laugh. "A little hard to shoot with an unarmed reconnaissance jet, wouldn't you say? Nice trick with the landing gear back there, but you won't get that chance again. Give it up, Drive. You don't have the stones for this fight. You don't have the commitment."

"There!" said Ryza and Ella at the same time, both pointing at a small installation coming into view below them.

They'd been flying over featureless scrub for the past few minutes, as if the terraformers had spent minimal effort on the asteroid's south pole. Now they swung low into a shallow depression, maybe an ancient meteor impact, towards a storm-grey metal group of cabinets and pipes built low to the ground.

So that's what the Peter Foundation's Graviton Device looks like, he thought. Precious few people had ever seen one. The Foundation gravity modifier at the Moon's south pole was guarded by a hundred-mile zone of instant death. The Foundation must have thought that Poundville's existing security measures were enough. This one was completely in the open.

Ryza needed a few moments. He wasn't going to get it, Joe knew, not with a horde of spacejets on their tail. Once they were on the ground they'd be blown to atoms.

Ella leaned over the back of his seat. "Thank you, Joe," she whispered, and the despondency was back. "For freeing me. For getting us this far. And for showing me just how evil my family has become."

She gazed down at him, dark brown eyes large and sparkling in the light of the sunset. Ryza was focused on the small structure, black wedge in his hand. Belltower, resigned to his fate, stared out at the growing twilight and the familiar stars. Somewhere behind them Novata and Lieutenant Talbot were still locked down. All of them waiting for him to decide.

He prodded Ryza in the thigh. "Get ready," he murmured. The monk hustled to the main cabin, followed by Ella. Then he toggled the comms. "You want commitment, Garfield? Then come and get it. You and me. No interference. No weapons. The winner walks away."

This time the laugh contained a note of incredulity. "A duel? Have you forgotten who trained you, boy? And what about you not trusting a word I say?"

"I don't," Joe replied evenly. As he worked the controls a lightness settled into his limbs, so much that he had to keep from smiling. "But they do. I don't think even you would break your word in front of the whole squadron."

The cockpit filled with silence. Joe knew it wouldn't last. He knew his enemy. His enemy was filled with pride. And pride would be his end.

"All right, Captain Drive. You and me. The winner walks away. Choose your ground." The comms buzzed with more commands and the horde of spacejets swung around into a wide, hovering circle of death, centered on the flat spot outside the installation. All the jets switched on their landing lights, illuminating the dark desert with a brilliant, harsh glare.

Joe set the Arrow down with one final gun of the engine, kicking up a thick plume of asteroid dust.

A rookie mistake. Unless you wanted cover.

"Go, go," he called towards the back, but Ryza already had the hatch open.

"Joe!" Ryza turned in the hatchway to face him. "Be ready! I have to pull the old wedge out before I slot the new one in. There'll be a delay." Then he ran for the group of grey cabinets and thick pipes that plumbed into the dirt. Ella was hot on his heels. They disappeared among the machinery.

Commitment is good, Joe thought as he strode for the hatch. But in the end, better intel wins the day.

Joe walked out of the hatch into the swirling dust, over to a clear spot, and waited. A spacejet separated from the ring of lethal firepower above him and dropped to the ground. Blinken Garfield swaggered out of the hatch and the jet lifted back to observation height again.

The commander looked a little the worse for wear, Joe thought. His face was marked with soot, one sleeve of his uniform burned. A cut over Garfield's right ear had scabbed over and stopped bleeding. "Sure you're up for this, Blink?" he called. "You've had a busy day."

"This?" He touched the scab. "Only a flesh wound. I've never been better. But you." He shook his head and advanced. "Just look at you, Captain. You've moped around the Moon for three years and it shows. You're fat, slow. You've got no wind in your sails. No commitment. You're standing still, Joe."

Garfield closed the last of the distance in a rush. Joe held his stillness for a moment longer, then sidestepped Garfield's initial grapple. Always Garfield's first move, and Joe had remembered. His mind was clear now, nothing in it but his training, firing his nerves and electrifying his reflexes. Garfield recovered his balance with a dancer's twist and was on him again.

He landed a solid fist under Garfield's ribs and heard the grunt. They struck and blocked a dozen times each. Joe felt his forearms bruise with the effort and began breathing hard. He dodged a leg sweep and got another shot in under Garfield's armpit, then used the momentary drop in Garfield's defences to land one on the man's ear.

"Yeah!" Garfield shouted, the grin wide on his face. "You're not completely wasted, Joe. Still remember a few things. But enough of the preliminaries."

And he came in. Hells, he was fast. Joe rocked back as a foot caught him on the thigh and a hand strike barely missed his nose, stinging his cheek instead. Garfield poured on the juice and Joe went on the defensive. He blocked and twisted and danced and, one at a time, Garfield landed blows. A rib shot took Joe's breath for a moment. Another kick made him dance on one foot for a beat too long, and he felt a fist graze his chin. Too close. Joe jumped back to regroup.

Garfield seemed to grow in front of him. "No

commitment," he said, square and unruffled. "You didn't have it then, and you don't now. Never paid attention in class, did you?" He raised his hands and waded in to finish things.

And strode up and over Joe, a wash of surprise taking over his face as his feet left the ground. Joe heard metal screech in the air above them as the ring of spacejets, exerting enough thrust to hover at station, suddenly found themselves launched for the stars. Several of them crashed into their neighbours.

Asteroid dust levitated off the ground to twinkle in the light from the spacejets. Away to his right, at the small installation, he heard Ryza and Ella laugh.

The monk had pulled the Poundville wedge out of the Foundation's gravity modifier. Ryza had changed the rules of engagement. Joe held perfectly still until Garfield was straight overhead, then sprang into the sky fist-first.

He slammed into Garfield's side as the big man tumbled helplessly in midair, the inertia pushing the man farther into the sky. In the opposite reaction, Joe was propelled back to the gravity-less asteroid. As soon as his feet touched earth he jumped again. This time he caught Garfield amidships, a solid solar plexus strike.

"Zero-G combat," he growled. "I paid attention for that."

Garfield had recovered and adapted. He spun around even as Joe's strike cost him his breath and grabbed Joe's wrist in a grip of steel. They hung in midair and twirled around each other, striking and blocking in a close-quarters, weightless brawl. Joe could smell the man's sweat, thick and predatory. Joe connected with a groin strike, then gave the commander's knee a vicious kick.

He smelled Garfield's aggression turn to fear.

Joe remembered the villages. Remembered the screams, the acrid smell, penetrating his cockpit even through the seals. He remembered his final flight, low and slow, watching the families and the markets and the houses evaporate as his bombs struck. Reprogrammed in mid-flight by Commander Blinken Garfield.

He remembered the assassin. Elite to the core, charged by Wheeler Pound and Garfield with an awful mission. To wreak havoc on the Moon with a small, black wedge.

The man in front of him had arranged that. Joe had removed the grin from Garfield's ugly meteor strike of a face. He pulled Garfield close to finish the job.

Garfield still fought, but Joe parried and returned the shots. A kidney, a rib, a glancing fist off Garfield's jaw. Joe was going to win.

Garfield got a finger free to jab the comms unit under his left ear. "Now, dammit!" he shouted to the squadron. In the same moment Joe heard Ryza's voice rise from the collection of grey pipes and boxes below. "Joe, now!"

Joe pulled Garfield as close as he could, placed one knee on the man's midriff and twisted. They spun in space as gravity returned to Poundville. Lots of gravity. Tons of it. His ears popped. He and Garfield fell for the ground as, all around them, spacejets plummeted out of the sky. A ring of crashes and explosions shook the asteroid's south pole.

Joe felt ribs break underneath him when he landed, knee first, with Commander Blinken Garfield between him and Poundville. The landing didn't stop there. A thousand-pound hand on his back slammed him all the way into the ground beside Garfield. His head struck dirt and tried to keep on going. He was helpless to stop it. The world went black as he struggled to take another breath.

He woke to Ryza and Ella carrying him by the arms. His feet dragged through the dust as they headed for the Celestial Arrow. All around them ruined spacejets burned, sending up a thick, choking smoke plume.

They could carry him. Gravity was back to normal. "Are you all right?" Ella was calling at him through the ongoing spacejet disaster. "That was amazing!" Ryza crowed.

He shook them off and stood, shaky on his legs and with a terrific headache, but operational. "You did that," he said, shaking Ryza's hand. "Monk, I like your idea of non-interference. Thanks."

Ella took her turn. She faced Ryza and shook his hand, giving the simple ceremony all the gravity it deserved. "Thank you, Senior Analyst Ryza. Oh behalf of the entire Resistance, thank you."

She was a mess. Her black hair was in tangles, her loose white blouse torn and covered in dirt. A cut on her cheek weeped a trickle of blood. They were all a mess, but they were standing. And Ella Pound had already moved into her new role as the official face of the Resistance.

"Yeah, all right," Ryza mumbled, overawed by the full presence of Ella's influence. "Not sure I'll be a Senior Analyst for long. This," he glanced at the carnage all around them, "goes a bit beyond my job description. But I'm pretty sure this isn't every spacejet on Poundville." He frowned over at Joe. "What do you think, Captain Drive? Can you get Ella back to the Moon before the rest of them get here?"

"I'm just Joe," he grumbled. Then he looked over towards the Arrow. "I could find the Moon with my eyes closed. What about you?"

Ryza's face hardened. "Drop me off at a Martian spaceport. This wedge doesn't get anywhere near the Moon, remember? I'm going to take it back to the Foundation that made it. And I'm going to let the Council know what's really going on."

Chapter 28

Ryza stood in the tiny lavatory of his Peter Foundation dorm and tightened the complex knot of his ceremonial sash. Too tight: he'd pulled it into a wrinkled mess. Uttering a most un-monklike curse, he undid it and tried again.

He'd announced his arrival the moment he landed, and been summoned to the Council to make his report. Not invited, as per the custom for Senior Analysts, by a messenger with a formal request. Summoned. By a temple guard. That was all the hint he needed to tell him what kind of meeting he was in for.

His report lay on the bed in its folder, thicker than most reports he'd filed before. He had a lot to say. A guard knocked on the door to escort him – escort him! – to the Pyramid. He snatched it up and exited the dorm, leaving the guard to catch up.

"Engineer Ryza, Senior Analyst of the Peter Foundation, you have been away from the home planet, observing. Now you have come to report. Tell us what you have seen." Uchenna wasn't smiling, and Ryza noted the lack of a welcoming tone in his voice. He scanned the rest of the seven

Sages and saw not an ounce of warmth.

"Chairman Uchenna, Sages of the Foundation Council, I have been watching and now I am home. Here is my report." He paused, then leaped in. "It is not good for humanity. It is worse for the Foundation."

Uchenna raised a wrinkled hand, his pink palm catching a ray of light from the white capstone overhead. Showman, Ryza thought. "Engineer Ryza. We, the Council, already know much of your travels and observations. And your actions. Unauthorized actions, which you were not approved to take, and which will have far-reaching implications. Give your report. But measure your words wisely."

"You're watching the watcher, is that it?" Ryza huffed, feeling the color rise in his cheeks. "I shouldn't be surprised. But you might take some time to watch each other, too. I presume you already know about Ella Pound's efforts to help the Resistance, her imprisonment, and her escape with the help of an ex-ISF soldier."

"And your help," one of the other Sages chimed in, to murmurs from the rest.

"Yes, my help. They needed it, too. Because Joe and Ella weren't just up against Wheeler Pound and his army. Turns out the Foundation was against them, too." He pulled the black wedge out of a pocket and dropped it on the lectern with a clack. He strained to observe all the Seven Sages at once as he did so, looking for any sign of astonishment, concern, or dismay. Anything, really. But they were all as if carved from stone.

Silence from the Council. So he continued. "You all know what this is. Do you know what it's calibrated for? To harm the Moon. This Graviton would have boosted the Moon's force to ten-X. We don't know what part of the Moon was the intended target. But everyone, everything not made of solid rock in the target zone, would have been crushed to dust." His voice had risen with his outrage, and he did nothing to calm it. The hall rang with his words. "Someone at the Foundation made this. Here, in the only place it could be made. I have no idea why. But it's evil, unspeakably so. You need to find whoever did this, Sages. That's the action you need to take. Now."

Uchenna's hand was raised again. "Engineer Ryza, enough. You found a rogue Graviton. What did you do with it?"

Ryza snorted. "I'm sure the Algorithm has already told you what I did. I used it to save our asses on Poundville. I helped get Ella Pound back where she could do some good in this messed-up Solar System."

The Chairman's face wrinkled with distaste, the lines ascending all the way to his bald head. "Correct. You acted, without direction and without authorization. Your gravity burst on Poundville, although brief, created a dozen sandstorms on Mars. One of them brought down an airship with an important politician on board, a woman with influence where we needed it. You say you helped free Ella Pound to do good work. So you know which work is good, and which is not?" Uchenna leaned forward, and for the first time Ryza saw real anger on the man's face. "So we no longer need the Algorithm, or the Prognosticator to interpret it? We no longer need Peter? We have Ryza now. Ryza will know what is good for all of us."

"No, that's not – I was just trying to restore some balance – helping the Resistance has to be right." Ryza found himself stumbling over his words. "I keep asking you what the Algorithm has to say. You give me nothing. So I have to guess for myself."

Another murmur went through the Council. "I put it to the vote," intoned Uchenna, and he looked around the crescent table. One by one, all the other Sages raised a palm, then turned their hand around. Uchenna turned his attention back to Ryza. "Engineer Ryza, Senior Analyst of the Peter Foundation. You were tasked to observe and report. To give the pilot Joe Drive a nudge into action. This you have done, faithfully and well. You were not tasked with taking action yourself. You were not tasked with interpreting events according to your own whims, and you never will be. You have told this Council that, in the absence of direction from the Sages or the Algorithm, instead of seeking our guidance you 'guessed for yourself.' These decisions are immature. They may have been harmful in ways the Algorithm has yet to determine. Engineer Ryza. Remove your sash."

He'd been expecting it. Still, his ears burned as he untied the knot, took off the red sash with the two gold stripes, and laid it next to his report on the lectern. Both the report and the sash sank out of sight. A moment later a new sash appeared. Red, as befit an Engineer. With one blue stripe.

"Engineer Ryza, Project Engineer of the Peter Foundation, don your sash." Uchenna paused while Ryza tied the knot, then continued. "This gives us no pleasure, Ryza. We need your skills, and you shall oversee important projects to further the Foundation's work. But you will give regular reports to your Analyst, and you will not travel off Earth unless authorized."

Ryza scowled, then nodded. At least they hadn't thrown him into the Peruvian desert. He waved a hand at the black graviton wedge, still occupying a corner of the lectern. "What about that?"

One of the other Sages spoke up. "What would you do, if it were returned to you?"

He snorted. "Smash it into a million pieces, that's what."

Uchenna almost smiled, but didn't quite make it. "Then,

Project Engineer Ryza, that is your first project. Destroy it. Return the shards to the vault. Then report to your Analyst for your next assignment."

Ryza picked up the wedge, which was still warm from being in his pocket. He'd get rid of this one evil. Then, in whatever spare time his new position afforded him, search out the evil that had made it. As he left the Council chambers he cast one last glance over his shoulder at the seven old men around their crescent table. Would his search lead back to this room?

Only the Algorithm knew for sure. And he wasn't even certain of that.

Chapter 29

Heaviside slumbered through the wee hours of the morning as Joe brought the Arrow in under cover of darkness. He set the craft down on the ridge overlooking the mine and made it shipshape while Ella took in the view. The trip back had been mostly quiet. Bellweather, Novata and Lieutenant Talbot had stayed on Poundville to help their comrades, and Ryza was off doing his monk thing. When the Arrow was put to bed he and Ella used the lonely transpo booth to fuzz back to Joe's apartment.

Ella wandered around, checking out the mountain-cabin decor of his main floor. "Looks different from this side," she commented as he found them a basic meal. "Warmer. More like a home. I like it."

He answered from the kitchen. A knot of discomfort was growing in his gut as she examined the apartment. Now that the mission was over, he had no idea what to do with her. He got the sense, once again, of just how different their worlds were. And how his had gotten small. "Well, it's not a palace, but it suits me. Listen, Ella, I like having you here, but we need to get you to the Resistance. Let them know what's going on. I steer clear of all that, so I don't know who to contact."

She paused, the ancient pistol from the mantelpiece in her hand, and gave him a funny look. Almost disappointed, he thought. Then she said, "I've already made the call. There's a cell here in Heaviside who will help me get to Venus and the headquarters of the Resistance, deep under the surface of the planet. The rebels actually have quite a thriving community there. I'll be safe with them. From there I can tell the Solar System what's really going on." A small smile touched her face. "I'm supposed to meet them at Stony's Bar and Grill. Think you can show me the way?"

"Hah!" Joe burst into a laugh, then felt the momentary amusement slide away. "That figures. Yeah, I know the place. But, uh, I can't get there."

He was spared further explanation by a soft chime from his doorplate. He checked the screen, then opened the door wide. Everest stood on his doorstep. But not barmaid Everest, in work clothes and a cook's apron. Her long hair was done in a complicated braid, matching the elegant knitted cords on her soft, cream pullover. She was wearing a skirt, and her shoes were genuine Earthside.

"Ms. Pound, my name is Everest," she said from the door. Then she turned on the barmaid's smile he remembered. "Hey Joe. Mind if I come in?"

Ella reached past him and guided Everest into the living room. As Ella passed by she winked. Actually winked. "Hey Joe," she whispered.

The glowing sign in the lava tube entrance to Stony's Bar said 'Closed For Private Function.' When they walked in Joe saw a group of people gathered around the bar, and Stony handing out drinks from one of the good bottles he kept behind the rail. Everyone turned to face them.

For the second time in a week, Ella's entrance made the

place go silent.

Ella took charge. Everest had brought her a change of clothes, but she'd elected to keep the smudges of the Poundville fight on her face, and she'd done nothing about the cut on her cheek. It would leave a small scar as it healed. A brilliant touch, Joe thought.

She walked down the three steps to a woman who had separated herself from the rest. "Sharaya Dustchild," she said, "I am Ella Pound. I'm here to help." The two embraced and a smattering of cheers and applause filled the room. Joe found himself applauding along with them.

The meeting became a celebration. Everest donned an apron over the soft pullover and kept the drinks moving. She brought Joe an Ion Burn. "Nice to have you back," she said, giving him a smile. "New and improved, from the looks of it." She ran a finger along the edge of a black eye, laughed and walked away. Joe held back on the edges of the party and watched.

Ella was a natural. She worked the room, meeting everyone, listening and talking in turn. All the attention was on her. Joe caught his name as she told the story of their escape, but tuned it out. He'd been there. The Ion Burn was good, and sent a pleasing warmth through his tired veins.

"You come here often?" Ella was at his shoulder, drink in hand and momentarily alone. "This is a crazy place. I have no idea where we are."

"That's the point," Joe said.

"We'll be leaving soon." She kept her gaze on the room and left the invitation lying between them. Waited to see if he would pick it up.

"Yeah, I guess you will. Life with the Resistance will be rough. You'll have a target on your back. Be safe over there, okay?"

She turned to face him. "Listen, Joe. You've had a quiet three years, but things are going to get hot now. On the outer planets, on the Moon here. Even on Earth, I think. The Peter Foundation aren't the only ones who can see what's coming. You were right. I can do some good here." She placed a hand on his shoulder, maybe the one place that didn't hurt. "So can you, if you want. The rebels have a difficult road ahead, even with my influence. They need you. Will you come with us? With me?"

It wasn't really a decision. Three years had come and gone since his ISF days, and his soul still felt bruised. He took a long breath, let it out. "I just want to be left alone," he said at last. "Have a nice adventure, Ella. Swing by if you're ever in the neighborhood."

She pursed her lips as if to say something, then they melted into a sad smile. "All right, Joe. Enjoy your retirement. You've earned it."

She leaned in and gave him a solid, slow kiss on the cheek, and then rose to leave. "Oh, yes," she paused and tapped the air over her wrists with her fingertips. His wallet buzzed. "In fulfilment of your contract, Mr. Drive. You broke me out of my father's prison, then saved me from my own."

He watched her gather with the rebel group, say goodbye to Stony and walk out. The Ion Burn was gone. He rose to leave, too. On his way to the door Stony called, "Hey, Drive."

Joe turned. Stony held out a business card. He took it.

"Suppose you can't promise me there'll never be any more trouble. I guess trouble's going to reach just about everywhere before this is through." Stony slung the towel off his shoulder, turned to his glasses and resumed polishing.

The grey light of a Heaviside morning washed the color out of The Shaft on the twenty-block walk back to his place. The Circadian dome over the city was set to transparent, and the light filtering through the high overcast was real, warm.

The transpo booths had long lineups in front of them, the morning shift headed for the mines. Joe looked at the people of his city, really studied them for the first time.

They didn't look happy. The Lowlifes in the lineups looked tired. A few of them barely concealed a simmering anger.

He watched the morning reels before finding bed. The rebel public influence team was already at work. Some of the reels, those most closely controlled by Pound Enterprises, showed nothing special. The rest were full of Ella's face as she broadcast news of her captivity, her narrow escape, and her Endowment's support of the Resistance. She never mentioned Joe, for which he was thankful. She also left out any mention of Ryza, the wedge, and messing with gravity. Sound tactics, he thought. Save the really evil news for later.

By the time he rotated back to a Pound Enterprises reel, old Wheeler had come up with his own story. Wheeler himself was on the screen, fury and hurt vying for dominance on his thin, raptor face. Ella had been kidnapped, he said, detained and brutally brainwashed by the rebels. The Home Alliance, in an unprecedented move, had given Wheeler full use of the Interstellar Space Force and free license to do what was needed to get his daughter back.

"And so it begins." Joe toasted the holo screen, drained his glass and went to bed, shutting his eyes against the future and the grey morning light.

The End

Get the first story

Long before Ella Pound showed up in his bar, Joe saved Slide (he goes by Simon now) from a horrible fate.

Midnight at Crater Quarry is only available to newsletter subscribers. **Sign up now** and you'll be first in line for new releases, insider offers and news from the writing life.

Head over to **triggerjones.com/newsletter** today.

Thanks for reading

We hope you enjoyed Book One in the Ion Burn series. Book Two, ***Atmosphere Meltdown,*** is available at an e-bookstore near you. Join our newsletter or follow Trigger Jones on Facebook to catch the launch of Book Three.

Tell your friends

Joe Drive loves stars. Especially the ones you leave where you bought this book online.

Say a few words, too! Reviews make a big difference to a story's success.

Tell your friends about ***Gravity Doesn't Lie.*** Mention it on your social network. Recommend it to your local library. Word of mouth is the best praise a book can get. It's serious rocket fuel.

Atmosphere Meltdown
Book Two in the Ion Burn series

Atmosphere Alert: Seek Pressurized Shelter Immediately

The worst alert to get on the back side of the Moon. When a mine accident in the crater jeopardizes Heaviside City's oxygen, Earth's Home Alliance blames it on Resistance sabotage. Joe Drive, ex-Space Force pilot, wants to ignore it all. He's done with the fight. But **a determined widow demands Joe's help** proving her husband was murdered to hide the truth. Joe reluctantly agrees to investigate.

The truth is worse than he imagined. **This was no accident.** The Home Alliance wants to take over the Moon, and **they'll kill an entire city to do it.** The streets fill with armed patrols, the Number 3 Mine goes on lockdown, and Joe and his friends are all over the holoreels as wanted terrorists. The tension on the streets has become a riot.

With the help of a rogue monk, a rebellious teen, a math geek and **a strange child living under the kitchen sink**, Joe must stop a man who would sacrifice a population as a means to an end. Or, for every soul in Heaviside City, **their next breath might be their last.**

Pick up *Atmosphere Meltdown* today:
https://books2read.com/atmospheremeltdown

Acknowledgments

No book gets written without a lot of help. We'd like to thank our beta readers, Deanna B, Mike C, and Brad J, for invaluable feedback that helped shape the story.

The crew at MiblArt did a fine job on the cover design, without which any book is just naked.

And thanks to the 20Booksto50K group for an avalanche of advice, instruction and inspiration.

Trigger Jones is the love child of thriller author Tony Berryman and mystery plot expert Juanita Rose Violini.

Juanita and Tony bring a dark sense of humour and a shared sense of the absurd to the Trigger Jones stories. They often hash out their plotlines and characters during long road trips. One rule of thumb: if an idea makes them both laugh, it goes in the book.

When not writing Trigger Jones stories, Tony works on thrillers. His first medical thriller, *The Night Nurse*, pits a massage therapist with an eye for patterns against the last nurse you'd ever want to meet. His second massage therapy thriller, *On Borrowed Time*, comes out in 2023.

Juanita is a full-time artist and mystery plot consultant. Her book *Almanac of The Infamous* is a collection of 365 unsolved mysteries and unexplained phenomena. *Cluetrail: From Whodunnit to Solution* is a step-by-step guide to crafting a fairplay mystery plot. You can find her artwork at Artfromtheoutpost.com. You can download murder mystery scripts or book a plot consultation at Mysteryfactory.com.